Gert Ledig (1921-99) was born in Leipzig and grew up in Vienna. At the age of eighteen he volunteered for the army and was wounded at the battle of Leningrad in 1942, later reworking his experiences in his novel *Die Stalinorgel* (*The Stalin Organ*) (1955). Sent back home, he trained as a naval engineer and was caught in several air raids. The experience never left him and led to the writing of *Vergeltung* (*Payback*) (1956). The novel's reissue in Germany in 1999 heralded a much publicized rediscovery of the author's work there.

Shaun Whiteside's translations from French, German and Italian include *Teeth and Spies* (Granta Books) and *Snow and Guilt* by Giorgio Pressburger. His translation of Lilian Faschinger's novel *Magdalena the Sinner* won the 1997 Schlegel-Tieck Prize.

GERT LEDIG

Payback

Translated from the German by
SHAUN WHITESIDE

Introduction by
Michael Hofmann

Granta Books
London

Granta Publications, 2/3 Hanover Yard, Noel Road,
London N1 8BE

First published in Great Britain by Granta Books 2003

A CIP catalogue record for this book
is available from the British Library.

1 3 5 7 9 10 8 6 4 2

Typeset by M Rules
Printed and bound in Great Britain by Mackays of Chatham PLC

Translator's note

The 'flak tower' or 'bunker' described in the novel is a massive four-storey concrete anti-aircraft shelter. These structures could hold several thousand people, and had on their roofs a platform supporting an anti-aircraft gun emplacement. Flak towers were built between 1943 and 1944 in Berlin, Hamburg and Vienna, where some can still be seen today.

I should like to thank the staff of the Imperial War Museum Library and Barbara Honrath of the Goethe Institute for their valuable help.

S.W.

Publisher's note

All names of characters in this book, as well as the date and time of the air-raid described in it, are invented. Any resemblance to members of the US Air Force that bombed Germany in 1944–5, or to German soldiers and civilians, is unintentional.

*Dedicated to a dead woman
whom I never saw alive*

INTRODUCTION
Mortal Slapstick:
An Essay on Gert Ledig

We believe in our justice, our punctuality, and – if they fail us –
then in our systems of retrieval. Little, we think, truly escapes
us. What, then, to make of the strange case of Gert Ledig, who
in 1955 very successfully published one novel, *Die Stalinorgel*
(The Stalin Organ – a military slang term for a multiple rocket
launcher), promptly translated into fourteen languages, followed that with two other books, *Vergeltung* (Payback) and
Faustrecht (Jungle Law) in 1956 and 1957, and shortly afterwards found that he no longer existed as an author?

Forty-four years later, in 1999, 2000 and 2001, these three
books were republished in Germany, to great interest and
acclaim. (Ledig had the satisfaction of knowing they were
scheduled, and he saw a proof of *Payback*, but he didn't live to
see publication; he died on 1 June 1999; perhaps not surpris-
ingly, he had turned his back on the literary scene anyway – if
he had ever faced it in the first place – and it would have
been a difficult thing for him to have experienced, after such
a break. He had carried on writing for a living, but articles for
technical journals.) His case is a little reminiscent of that of

Wolfgang Koeppen (whose 'postwar trilogy' was published in 1951, 1953 and 1954, and whom Ledig certainly read, and who in turn admired Ledig), but there are clear differences too: Ledig, one feels, was a writer by accident (the accident of overwhelming experience), and for a time only; Koeppen was a writer through and through, even when he wasn't writing. Moreover, Koeppen was sustained by his publishers, even through long silences, and never entirely disappeared from view, while Ledig was never with anyone for more than one book. None of this, of course, does anything to alter the fact that his 'disappearance' was regrettable and mistaken, and that his return to public awareness, in Germany, and now in Britain, is much to be welcomed.

Instrumental in his rediscovery, but only obliquely, was the late W.G. Sebald, who in 1997 gave a series of lectures in Zurich on bombing and literature. I say obliquely, because *Payback* formed no part in his talks, the burden of which, ironically, was to identify and to complain at the absence of writing on this huge and widely shared trauma – and if Sebald, the brilliant researcher, was unaware of him, that is a powerful indication of how thoroughly Ledig's reputation had disappeared. It was in the ensuing public and media debate that attention was finally drawn to Ledig and his books, and republication was set in motion. When Suhrkamp published *The Stalin Organ* in 2000, it appeared in a wrapper hailing 'the rediscovery of a major author'; while Sebald, in the version of his lectures that was revised for publication, devotes a couple of pages to *Payback*, praising it for its exemplary toughness and uncompromisingness.

As Ledig never made it into any sort of pantheon, information on him is sketchy and a little dry. He was born in

1921 in Leipzig, grew up in Vienna, and volunteered for the Wehrmacht at the age of eighteen. He got into trouble for 'inflammatory talk' – an interesting detail in view of his subsequent ideological convictions – and for a time, in 1942, he was in a punishment unit. He was twice wounded fighting the Russians, losing two fingers on his right hand, and part of his lower jaw, and was sent back to Germany, where he worked in the civilian war effort, as an engineer in Munich. This gave him a wholly new perspective on war, the passive, defensive, largely civilian experience of being bombed from the air. After the War, he did various jobs, including, oddly, working for the US Army as an interpreter and translator (the English in his books is not, by German standards, particularly good). *The Stalin Organ* was sent to fifty publishers before being accepted by a rather apprehensive Claassen Verlag, who were astonished by its critical and international success. Ledig found himself courted by parts of the West German literary establishment, but a feeling of not belonging, reinforced by his unease – with his disability – at speaking in public, kept him from ever succumbing to its advances. He was, moreover, rather to the left of most of his admirers, espousing the German Communist Party's pro-East German line. It is more than likely that his failure to stay the course with publishers or West German critical opinion has something to do with the devious and unnegotiable domestic German politics of the Cold War period. (The Stasi thought briefly of running him as an agent, but he doesn't seem to have satisfied them either; they had him watched by, among others, Christa Wolf – material there, I would have thought, for a play or radio drama.) One has a sense of a difficult man, with unsatisfied ideological appetites, uncomfortable with the

career and the milieu in which his literary success had briefly
landed him.

Gert Ledig's three books – a triad, really, rather than a trilogy – are all to do with the War, and each of them offers a
remarkably pure and bleak perspective on it. *The Stalin Organ*
is about the fighting in Russia – which, it seems safe to say,
was probably the most vicious and destructive in the entire
history of human conflict. *Payback* takes a single hour –
seventy minutes, to be absolutely precise, a 'bomber's hour',
perhaps – from the firebombing of an unnamed German city,
as it might be Hamburg or Dresden, where the density of
explosions caused the air to combust. Both books are utterly
radical in their pursuit of horror, sliding from scene to scene,
pockets of pain and mutilation that are almost beyond narra-
tive. They are existential writing on the very edge of nihilism,
the mostly unnamed protagonists (the word seems an over-
statement) scrabbling through a world that is worse than
Dante or Goya or Dix or Beckett. (An early working title for
Payback was *Inferno*.) There is almost no contrast with the
insects, the flies and cockroaches that put in an occasional
appearance. Life is cut away to a residual biological functioning,
such things as weather and landscape to an ambient death. It
is roulette, but where the bank claims all thirty-seven spaces
for itself. 'We must love one another, or die', wrote the
humanist W.H. Auden; Ledig's implicit counter is 'We must
kill one another *and* die.' There is no consolation of form or
language or meaning. Even something as stark and disciplined
as Ernst Jünger's World War I book, *Storm of Steel* – allied,
admittedly, with a persistent human address – seems a far
cry. Ledig *is* literature, but literature compacted of action and
nerve. I can't imagine any account containing a greater

measure of what one might call neural event; higher brain activity is ruthlessly stripped out. The third book of the triad, *Jungle Law*, to mention it briefly, is somewhat different, set in the post-War atmosphere of vets, spivs and whores, under the American occupation; it has quite an American feel to it – it is easy to imagine Rob and Edel and Shark played by Bogart and Cagney and Mitchum – a rare piece of German *noir*. Its clipped speech and unexpected dramaturgy seem like a departure for Ledig, until one recalls the clever and convincing rape-sequence in *Payback* – and then one thinks that Ledig might have had it in him to be a writer after all, and to have gone beyond the grisly *données* of the War in his first two books.

Ledig's novels – the first two in particular – reclaim the subject of war from, on the one hand, films and cartoons, and on the other, history and statistics. It is no longer a matter of heroism, valour, face-to-face engagement with the enemy. There are no clean holes, no ketchup wounds, no tidy explosions. Instead, suicides, punishment shootings, attempted surrender, contemplated murder. There are no classic lines of engagement, but, in *Payback*, strata of death at different altitudes, and, in *The Stalin Organ*, a strange, Dantesque interpenetration of the foes, with detached units like the circles in a mandala. The elements are enlisted – earth, air, fire – but the solid air and liquid fire of a new physics. Viscous fluids seep and trickle everywhere, Mary Douglas's 'matter out of place'. The human figure is diminished to the 'Tree of Fluids' of Jean Dubuffet's 1950 painting in the Tate Modern. Compound nouns bespeak a new monstrosity: *Bombenteppich*, bomb-carpet, *Steinfontäne*, stone-fountains, *Gewehrmündungen*, rifle-mouths, *Metallzahn*, metal tooth, *Rauchvergiftung*, smoke-poisoning, *Luftmine*, flying-bomb. Odd collocations appear, a man pulls a paper bag full of Iron Crosses out of his desk drawer, a cripple is given an apple and stows it away in a suitcase next to a plaster mock-up of his foot. A new rationality has evolved too, where Russian labourers beg to be shot, a doctor is a bullying sadist, a Hitler Youth boy has a vast, Homeric appetite for fighting and murder, where Strenehen, the American pilot in *Payback*, takes off his shoes before walking across a patch of broken glass. Life and death are no longer an antinomy, but a sort of continuum, where people die incrementally, and their bodies continue to be pulverized and spattered in a gruesome literal anticipation of the term 'overkill'. (Both *Payback* and *The Stalin Organ* begin with corpses receiving insult after injury.) There is at times a medieval or Mexican morbidity about proceedings, a soap opera from old bones.

This gruesomeness, astonishingly, and I think deliberately, shades into comedy. It is a comedy of errors, of mortal slapstick, of being tickled to death, or by death. A peculiarly raw irony operates, too broad, almost, to deserve the name (the multiple deaths would be an example, the bombing of the cemetery, the shooting of corpses). It is a mechanical, pervasive, inevitable irony, a function not of calculation or design or timing, but of an overplus of brute death. Sonia Shalyeva in *The Stalin Organ* is enlisted to serve as a nurse in a dressing-hut. She is told by the doctor to hold the hands of the wounded while he operates on them. The next man has no hands; she holds him by the head. A little later a wounded man 'stands up' (the German verb *aufgerichtet* is also the word applied to the male erection); at which point he sees that he has been emasculated and screams with loss. In *Payback*, it is the sand falling 'tenderly' between the breasts of the raped girl suffocating in a hole in the ground, or the lieutenant reclaiming his prosthesis from the Russian labourer's hand when they get back on their feet after diving for cover. It may not be funny, but it is certainly comedy, albeit at its very blackest.

The challenge of war as a subject – perhaps especially modern, mechanised war – is to get us to *feel* it, sharply and viscerally, not merely to know it or think it, in a dull and droning way. To my mind, Ledig has succeeded, to an intolerable, perhaps even an unrivalled degree. It is easy to suppose him artless, as many even of the admiring German reviews seem to do. In fact, though, he shows rigour, imagination and judgement in his short, four-, five-, six-word sentences, his insistently claustrophobic scenes, his dispassionate ability to view the action from every side – German, Russian, American, civilian, soldier, bomber, ack-ack gunner, officer, enlisted man – his uncanny ability to offer just enough in the way of individuation to get us as readers to *care* about the vestigial human beings he sets before us, rather than (as we would like to do) push them away from us as routine instances of horror and carnage. Reading him, we are confronted both with the magnitude of awfulness – four hundred bombers with their 'payload' of two trains' worth of explosive – and the detail. No 'Tolstoyan light', as Wolfgang Koeppen beautifully put it in a letter to Ledig's editor, plays over 'the utter darkness of his battle scenes. He has reached the point of irreducible finality.'

Michael Hofmann
London, October 2002

Payback

13:01 Central European time

Suffer the little children to come unto me. –

When the first bomb fell, the blast hurled the dead children against the wall. They had suffocated in a cellar the day before. They had been laid in the graveyard because their fathers were fighting at the front and their mothers were still missing. Only one was found, but she was crushed under the rubble. That was what payback looked like.

A little shoe soared high with the cascade of earth thrown up by the bomb. It didn't matter. It was already torn. When the earth pattered down again, the sirens began to wail. It sounded like the start of a hurricane. A hundred thousand people felt their hearts pounding. The city had been burning for three days, since which time the sirens regularly began to wail too late. It was as though they were being set off like that deliberately, on the grounds that people needed time to live in between being bombed to pieces.

That was the beginning.

Two women across the road from the graveyard wall let go of a handcart and ran. They thought the graveyard wall would be safe. They were mistaken.

Suddenly engines rumbled in the sky. A sharp arrow-fall of magnesium incendiaries bored hissing into the asphalt. A second later they burst open. Where asphalt had been, flames crackled. The handcart was blown over by the blast. The shaft flew into the air, a child rolled out of a blanket. The mother by the wall did not scream. She didn't have time. This was no children's playground.

Next to the mother stood a woman burning like a torch. She was screaming. The mother looked on helpless, then she too was on fire. It raced up her legs, up her thighs, to her body. She felt it happening, then she collapsed. A shock wave exploded along the graveyard wall and in that moment the road burned too. Asphalt, stones, air.

That was what happened by the graveyard.

Inside it was different. The day before yesterday the bombs had unearthed things. Yesterday they had covered them back up again. And today's events were still to come. Even the rotten corpses in the soldiers' graves didn't know what was going to happen, and they should have. On their crosses it said: You did not fall in vain.

Perhaps they were cremated today.

The lieutenant had had his left hand amputated. The hand was one thousand five hundred miles away from the city in the lime-pit of the field hospital at El Alamein. It had rotted there. Now the lieutenant had a prosthetic hand, an anti-aircraft battery behind the graveyard, ten ex-soldiers and the graduating class of the Humanist Grammar School.

The incendiaries flew three miles through the air. They burst onto his concrete bunker. They had been launched by Sergeant Strenehen, later described as:

A human being.

There were plenty of those. When Strenehen saw the flames surging across the graveyard, he was pleased for a second. He had chosen that target in the hope that the bombs would hit nothing but corpses. He didn't know that sixty minutes later one of his own men would be beaten to death with shovels because of it.

During that hour, or after it, still more people were killed. An unborn child in its mother's body, by the collapsing wall of a house. A French prisoner of war by the name of Jean-Pierre, killed by a rifle butt. Six pupils from the Humanist Grammar School near the anti-aircraft battery, killed by the exploding barrel of an anti-aircraft gun. Several hundred nameless others.

It wasn't worth mentioning. During those sixty minutes people were torn apart, crushed, suffocated. Anyone left would wait till tomorrow.

Later someone said: It wasn't as bad as all that. There are always a few people left.

Although he wasn't near the latrine of the US Air Force plane, Sergeant Strenehen had thrown up anyway. He had flown through several hurricanes without throwing up. When the flaps of the bomb-bay opened, he vomited again and again.

And the opening of the flaps was a mechanical process. It was initiated by the mechanism of the sighting device. This precision instrument calculated angle of elevation, trajectory, back-drift, ballistic correction. It armed the fuses, operated the bomb-racks. The invention of the guillotine was primitive in comparison.

Sergeant Strenehen's squadron was the path finder. The first wave followed seventy miles behind. Four hundred bombers carried the contents of two freight-trains filled with explosives through the air.

The sun glinted on their wings. Clouds sat on the horizon. The engines roared, and thirty miles behind the first wave the second followed.

I

I, Maria Erika Weinert, was born on 4 July 1925 in Marburg on the Lahn. After attending secondary school and business school, I got a job as a clerk. For that reason I left my parents and lived in a fairly large city between the Rhine and the Elbe.

My favourite colour was blue. I wore my long hair in a roll at the nape of my neck. Had it been possible, I should have liked to learn to dance. But when I was between the ages of fourteen and eighteen, dancing was not allowed. For a year I wrote letters to a soldier whom I never saw. My greatest experience was a summer holiday by the sea. Our room was just by the beach.

At that time I was still a child. There were roses in my parents' garden. One day at school I was allowed to play Snow White, in spite of my blonde hair. I never forgot the feeling I had when I stood on the stage in our school hall in front of all those people.

I had two summer dresses. One of them was white with a print of big cornflowers. I didn't have an evening dress. I have drunk sparkling wine twice in my life. Once at my confirmation. The second time when the soldier I used to write to sent me a parcel from France.

The needle on the altimeter quivered like the pointer on a set of scales. The puff of cloud from a flak burst hurtled towards the cockpit windscreen and dispersed on the glass. They were flying through the midst of the barrage curtain. Wisps of smoke hung in the air. The only sound came from the engines. They couldn't hear the explosions.

Ohm stared over the captain's shoulders at the instrument panel. If the plane went down, he was twenty feet from the nearest opening. Unless a shell exploded in the fuel tanks, in which case he would burn to death. He thought: My grandfather picked cotton. My father went to war alongside the whites. They put up a memorial to him in Harlem: I am a free man.

His feet trembled. The floor's rubber surface muffled everything. The trembling wasn't coming from the engines.

While my wife and my son Abraham were sleeping, he thought, it happened. The sea lies between me and my wife, and the strange woman wasn't even of my race. The Lord says: I will visit your sins upon you unto the third and fourth

generation. He knew what that meant. His large hands settled
on the ammunition boxes to pray: Forgive me, I couldn't help
it. I am weak and in Thy power. When he looked away from
the rev counter he saw the horizon.

A fountain spread on the ground below them. It consisted
of tracer fire collapsing back upon itself. They were flying too
high for light flak. The shells weren't reaching them.

Jesus, he prayed. My wife irons clothes for strangers.
People say she's a hard worker. Abraham's nearly seven. My
father got a memorial. It was supposed to be made of bronze.
The money they collected only stretched to plaster. The plaster was supposed to be covered with paint. I have painted it
year after year.

He prayed: Forgive me. If this is my final hour, I will die
with a sin upon me.

It was time to mark their targets. He didn't care. He hoped
no fighter planes would come. His thoughts refused to obey
him. At that moment nothing was as important as praying.
Hands folded, he mumbled away to himself.

A voice said: 'Ohm, you take Strenehen's place. I want to
talk to him.'

Captain Lester was talking on the intercom, and it was
coming through on the headphones. Prayers were over.

'Yes, sir!'

He turned around. Across the wings he saw the nose of the
next plane. In passing he touched the second pilot's shoulder,
then he was out of the cabin.

The sick woman lay in bed.

She was so swollen that she barely had the strength to
breathe. Her mattresses were crooked, her grey hair loose,

and there was sweat on her forehead. Christ looked down at her, a mild-faced man in a long robe, standing on a cloud. The print hung in a frame on the wall. The sirens had fallen silent. The son of God couldn't move.

The door opened and a woman dressed in mourning and a girl walked in, carrying a chair. Together they lifted the patient out of bed.

They took hold of her without a word. A blonde curl fell over the girl's forehead, wind blew through the open window, a distant, dull roar came in. When the sick woman was settled on the chair, they carried it outside. The crumpled bed and the print were left behind.

The girl and the woman carried their load downstairs, one step at a time. At the next landing they had to rest. Salvoes echoed between the houses at the back. The woman and the girl put the chair down on the landing. It moved each time the guns fired.

A hundred steps to go to the cellar door.

The girl put her hand to her brow. Sweat was running down her back. The sick woman groaned. She stretched out her swollen arm, waved her hands in the air and showed the other two a cross made of iron.

'My son,' she sighed.

'Not now!'

The girl leaned forward. The strap of her dress slipped, resting on her collarbone. Where her fingers touched the sick woman's arm, they left an imprint.

The girl pushed the woman's arm back.

'Let's leave her where she is,' the other woman said suddenly.

'Here?'

The girl turned away. A shard of glass fell out of the window frame. It shattered on the floor.

'Yes, here.'

A blanket covered the sick woman's legs. The girl looked at it.

'All right, then.'

'Will she cry?'

The girl replied, 'Of course she will.'

The cross slid from the blanket and fell on the floor. The sick woman's puffy arm swept through the air in search of it. The girl picked up the cross and gave it back to her.

'Take it!'

The woman answered, 'It's too risky for us.'

'But it would be cruel!'

A blast of air pressure whistled through the window. Shrapnel rattled on the rooftops. The girl and the woman bent low at the same time. They picked up the chair; it wobbled.

A groan came from the sick woman's chest, then she toppled forwards. Down the stairs, one step at a time, head first, her body thumping on the steps. Only at the next landing did she come to a stop and lie with her legs splayed.

In the dark, the lieutenant collided with the concrete. He was shivering. Whenever he sat in the dark he shivered. The cold crept up the ground into his feet and through his belly to his back. He felt his sweat drenching his shirt.

Just for something to do, he was opening his mouth, when a voice said:

'Enemy formation keeping radio silence!'

Drops of water dripped from the ceiling and fell on to his hand. He raised his foot and touched the table with it.

'Do you want me to open the door?' somebody asked.

'No,' he answered quickly, 'it isn't over yet.'

The wall felt wet. There wasn't much light where the wireless operator was sitting. He waited until his eyes could make something out, but he couldn't make anything out at all. The darkness was all around him. Somewhere a watch was ticking. He thought: The dead don't need watches. He had taken the watch even though the corpse was already rotting. The crackling from outside grew fainter. Someone drummed on the table with his fingers. In the wireless operator's headphones an American voice said loudly: '*Reporting position!*'

'Now,' whispered the wireless operator, and the drumming of the fingers on the table stopped.

The lieutenant automatically leaned forwards. The watch went on ticking. It was counting the seconds.

'That,' declared a voice from the table, 'that means nothing. The formation could still change its flight path.'

'Position?' asked the lieutenant.

'Forty miles west,' the radioman announced.

'What time is it?'

A match flared up. The lieutenant was dazzled. For a fraction of a second he saw the bare light-bulb hanging from the ceiling.

The voice from the table said: 'Two minutes past one. The train should be leaving now.'

The match went out. It was as dark as before.

'What train?' asked the wireless operator.

'The one carrying my wife and child.'

The operator pushed his chair back. 'They should have been sent out of town long ago.'

Outside on the concrete a jet of flame fizzled out. Three

stones thudded on the iron door, one after another. It sounded like a signal. A voice blared in the headphones, speaking English:

'*Train station! Bridge! Give a description!*'

'They're marking their targets,' said the lieutenant. The light-bulb dangling from the ceiling started to glow. The crackle of phosphorus fell silent. A smell of smoke came from the door.

'Why don't you sound the alarm?' asked the voice from the table.

'It's always the same,' the wireless operator explained. 'We're part of the stealth battery. Our order to fire only comes at the very last moment.'

The light-bulb started to flicker, then blinked out again. The lieutenant looked over towards the wireless operator.

'Position report?'

'Forty miles west!'

The voice at the table said: 'You know what "*train station*" means?'

'Yes.'

All at once the light-bulb sprang into brilliant light. It dazzled all three of them, the wireless operator, the lieutenant and the man in civvies. He leapt to his feet and asked: 'Can I go to the station?'

Without turning around, the lieutenant replied: 'That's forbidden!' The stump of his arm ached. He looked at the floor in front him. When he raised his head, he was looking into a mirror. The best cure for compassion. He thought: If I let him go he'll never come back. He had a cut on his chin, with a scrap of paper on it to staunch the blood. It had crusted now. He tore it off, and it started to bleed again. As he considered his face in the mirror, he thought about the schoolboys. Maybe it was better to have blood on your chin than paper.

Strenehen leaned on the bomb racks. Above him was the shaft leading to the gun turret. He looked down on the city through the observation window. A layer of haze hung between plane and earth. Muzzle-flash blazed through it. It shone like spotlights, except that the light was lethal.

The haze parted. Railway tracks converged on the ground far below and were swallowed by the station building. Dots streamed from tiny wagons. A swarm built up against an invisible barrier, formed a solid patch. One direct hit in there and it would all change colour. It would turn red, the colour of meat. The screams wouldn't reach the sky. They were flying four miles high.

Rows of houses lined up side by side. A square. Rubble. The outline of a flak tower. And then they were flying over the graveyard again. Balls of cotton-wool grabbed at the plane; it was dangerous for them to be so close. When Strenehen entered the cabin, he saw the quivering needle on the altimeter.

'Sir, you wanted to talk to me?'

'Intercom,' the captain replied. 'Plug yourself in. I'm not going to yell my head off just for you.'

'Yes, sir.'

Strenehen lifted the leather helmet from his chest and put it over his head. A heavy flak shell burst near the tail. It bent the wings forwards for a moment, there was a coughing in the air between the propellers, and then the plane was horizontal again, as though nothing had happened.

The captain's voice said on the headphones: 'You've

deliberately dumped our load on the graveyard. I expect an explanation!'

The figures, the ammunition crates and the four-barrelled flak gun were all in bright daylight. The gun pointed its barrels towards the sky. Sun fell on the platform. There were no shadows between heaven and earth. The bare colossus of the bunker loomed above all the rooftops. Smoke, not steam, rose from the street. The clouds didn't reach to the bunker's fourth storey. The figures stood on the flat roof, and beneath their feet people were breathing. Not a sound penetrated the concrete.

'Eat your chocolate now!' the gun commander ordered.

He looked up, to where the squadron was. The twelve bombers passed beyond the bunker. The roar of the engines faded. Wind brought a wall of soot from the graveyard. With luck, it would cover everything.

The loader said: 'You shouldn't eat before an air-raid.' He added: 'My dad said it was in case you got hit in the belly.'

Above the roof there were sounds like gongs being struck. A heavy battery was opening fire, over to the north.

'How old are you?' the gun commander asked.

'Fifteen.'

Little clouds formed in the sky where the squadron was flying. One of the bombers appeared to wobble, but it was just an illusion. The plane stayed in formation, and in the air.

'Eat your chocolate now!' repeated the gun commander. He thought: I hope it isn't your last. He scratched at the concrete with his boot, at a red patch. The patch was twelve hours old. There was no water on the concrete roof.

'If those are your orders, corporal,' said the loader.

'Eat up!'

The squadron emerged unexpectedly into the sky above the railway station. Black dots fell from the machines and exploded in the air. Banners of smoke formed where they burst. The gun commander thought: Chocolate contains caffeine. He took a piece, too. As he ate, he looked suspiciously into the boys' eyes.

They chewed obediently. Their helmets kept slipping over their faces.

'Tighten your chin-straps!' he ordered.

'Yes, sir!'

They answered in chorus. They obediently did as he ordered. That was the worst of it.

Now, he thought, if I were to give them the order: Go and jump into the road . . .

The salvoes from the battery suddenly rang out like the bellows of an animal. He waited for splinters, but none came yet. Only the wall of soot pushed its way closer. There was no need for its protection: the bombers weren't interested in an anti-aircraft gun.

'Why haven't we fired?' asked the loader.

'We only shoot at fighter-planes.' He looked through his visor. The wall of soot was drifting higher. It blocked his view. He saw roofs between the mount and the barrels, just roof-beams, with the shingles blown off. Not fifty yards away stood the charred skeleton of an apartment block. It was a mystery that it didn't collapse.

'Do you want to relieve yourselves?'

He thought: It has nothing to do with getting hit in the belly.

The engine noise mounted again. A single gun began to fire near the barracks. The shots roared out hollowly. His gunners went willingly to the edge of the platform. They relieved themselves. From sixty feet below came the sound of splashing on stones. There was no one in the street. The platform had no railings. An iron ladder led down from the rim. He thought: The place of execution has no portal.

'When it gets going,' he shouted, 'think about your work and don't just stare into the sky!'

Splinters twittered through the air. Caught unawares the gunners ducked down, startled. They stood back up, wide-eyed.

'Yes, corporal!' all four answered and fastened their trousers. There was no point explaining anything more to them. They would forget it all. The wall of soot seethed over the edge of the platform. By the time the squadron passed over them for a second time, they were standing in darkness. A black layer settled on the sights. The engine noise grew louder. The squadron had already flown past them, but the four were as green as children. They ducked under the gun and clung to the footplates.

'My God,' he said. He tasted soot on his tongue and fell silent.

By the time the clouds had passed by, his hands were black. He blew the sights clean. It couldn't be long now. Smoke signals hung in the air all over the city, purple flashes in the sunlight. In the station a train let off steam; it rose snow-white to the sky. The firing from the battery to the north intensified. Splinters fell across the neighbouring rooftops. A tile shattered, slipped from the roof, hurtled into the street, smashed onto the cobbles. From the barracks a red balloon rose into the sky.

The loader whispered: 'What's that?'

'Drift measurement!'

The gun commander heard a faint rumble on the horizon. It cut through the squadron's engine noise, through the dull reports of the guns and through the silence.

'Time to strap ourselves in!'

He bent down and reached for a strap that dangled from the gun. He wrapped it around his belly.

This time the loader obeyed immediately.

The windows were open. Herr Cheovski stood by the table in the living-room and gazed out. Not moving a muscle, he looked at the façade of the house opposite, at a row of windows, all without glass. It looked frozen, lifeless. He was wearing his patent leather shoes and his dark suit.

'I think they're coming,' said his wife. She was sitting beside the window, legs crossed. She held a lace cloth in her hand. He had never seen her so still.

'Yes.' He looked at the grandfather clock. The pendulum swung back and forth. The explosions of the anti-aircraft shells, the roar of the engines, the firing of the guns; it was all louder than the clock.

He said: 'Let's go and stand in the middle of the room.'

'If you think that's best.'

The lace cloth slid from her hand and floated on to the parquet. All he could do was pick it up. The floor was freshly buffed. When she stood up, he held out his hands to her. She was wearing her brocade evening dress.

'Let's go and stand by the table.'

'Yes, Dessy.'

She went and stood facing him across the table. He looked

into her eyes. Above them the chandeliers began to tremble. A piece of paint flaked off and floated down. It fell on to the white tablecloth. Roses on damask. The last time they had used it was when their eldest was promoted to captain. *Permission to refill glasses, Captain!* Walter's voice rang in his ears through the noise of the engines. Walter couldn't make any requests now, and the dead don't drink.

It never ended. He ran his hand over his eyes. The wine-glasses glittered in the display cabinet. A crack ran across the wall. She had dusted everywhere.

'The paintings?' he asked, when he looked at the empty walls. 'Did you put the paintings . . . ?'

'Let's not talk about that.'

A ray of sunlight slanted through the window. The parquet gleamed.

'I was just thinking,' he said.

'What?'

'Let's leave everything as it was.'

Her hands stroked the lace cloth. 'I burned them. It's better that way.'

'Of course, Dessy.'

He didn't know what else to say in reply. Their agreement not to talk about it paralysed every word. A window-pane exploded with a faint pop. The glass tinkled, Frau Cheovski flinched.

'It's nothing.' He tried to smile. A strenuous task that he had to force himself to perform, and he still couldn't do it. Her eye went to the tablecloth. 'Call me Dessy again!'

'Of course.'

'It's a long time since you called me that.'

'A lot has changed.' Without looking at the clock he knew

that the hand was moving. Time was running out. It had come too suddenly. The street lay deserted. They were the only ones remaining.

'Do you think so?' she asked.

'Of course.'

The façade on the other side blocked his view of the sky. Empty window-sockets. A hundred eyes gazing this way. At the formal white table, the empty patch on the wall. Frau Cheovski suddenly asked: 'What about a game of bridge?'

'Bridge! With two hands? You know that's impossible.'

'It is?' Her head lowered slightly. 'Please, fetch the cards.'

'Dessy, honestly, it's pointless.'

The parquet floor trembled.

Herr Cheovski was afraid the chandeliers might come loose. A childish fear, because that was how it would start.

'So you won't?'

'Dessy!' Surprised, he looked into her face. 'You've put on make-up!'

'I have. Do you think I'm too old for it?'

Neither of them spoke, until he shook his head. He heard himself saying: 'No, it's just been a long time.'

'Will you do as I ask?'

'Two hands! It won't work!'

'Let's play four hands,' she answered. 'I'll play with Walter, you play with Rudolf.'

He said: 'I don't think we've got the cards any more.'

'Yes we have.'

He asked: 'Where?'

'In the sideboard.' She swept the grains of sand from the tablecloth with her fingers. 'Near the wineglasses.'

'All right, then.' He turned around. He slowly walked the

three paces from the table to the buffet. He was making an effort to fulfil a wish. An illusion. He thought: time is passing. Time is certainly passing.

'I'm sorry,' Strenehen managed to say in reply, when a shadow emerged from the clouds and stooped as fast as a hawk on the bomber.

The turret-gunner cried: 'A German!' He was from Illinois. He was very proud of his teeth. Every day he wrote letters, always with the same ending: Mom, don't worry about me! A lot of use that was to him right now.

The eleven men in the plane heard the sound of his death through his microphone. He whimpered like a child for that split second, then he fell silent. His death was simple.

Fortunately for the bomber the German had been too late opening fire. The fighter's cannon shot too high, but the scatter of machine-gun fire hit the turret. Armour-piercing ammunition smashed straight into the swivel of the gun mounting. The butt of the machine gun slipped from the turret-gunner's shoulder, smashing into his jaw. Almost painlessly he lost thirty teeth. An explosive round ripped through his chest and shredded his lung through his ribs. The wound gaped from his right collar-bone to his left nipple. Half a gallon of blood gushed out. It splashed down on Strenehen, who leapt startled from the cockpit to the turret-shaft.

Captain Lester called: 'Watch out!'

He meant the fighter, not the blood, but the German was already vanishing among the clouds.

Ohm crouched beside the horizontal magazines. He muttered: 'Jesus! Jesus!' His face was pale grey. Everyone could hear his singsong voice. Strenehen kicked him in the face, quite unintentionally. The corpse lay doubled up in the opening. As Strenehen swung into the turret-shaft, he had to push it away with his arms outstretched. He clutched warm flesh. He was holding a piece of windpipe between his fingers. When he heaved his torso into the turret, the wind was lashing through the shattered windscreens. It dispersed the blood and blew it into his face. The lenses of his spectacles turned dark. He imagined there was a sweetish taste on his lips. He ran the back of his hand over his glasses, knelt on the corpse, shoved the mount into the gun-ring, hastily cleaned up the windscreen. He had nothing but his handkerchief to wipe with. A gift from Bardly Parish Church to its soldiers. It was too small for all that blood. When he had sorted everything out, he pushed the dead man's legs through the shaft and let him slide down. Right in front of Ohm's feet. He thought: Let him clear up. If the German came now, it would be payback time.

The corpse somersaulted away below him, and the German came. This time he had no cloud cover. Even so, he didn't change his tactic. He came like an arrow from the side, towards the nose of the aircraft. Strenehen knew at once what the German was trying to do. The bomber's weak point was just behind the cockpit. A shell from the fighter's cannon in there and they would explode in mid-air.

The first to hit the other was the winner.

The two planes hurtled towards one another. If the fighter didn't swerve they would crash head-on. They came closer.

Now, thought Strenehen, and pulled the trigger. The German was in his sights. The twin machine guns worked precisely. He aimed at the pilot. Not one shot missed. Threads of light flashed towards their target.

He'll die quickly, he thought. Faster! He imagined he was counting the shells. Sixty rounds a second.

Suddenly the other man's tail unit was over his head. It flashed over the turret. The hull. A shadow, end of shadow, sky. They hadn't touched each other. The German hadn't fired.

Strenehen turned the turret around, but he didn't need to fire. Two hundred feet behind him the fighter tipped over. It fell away, into infinity. Into the middle of the city.

Strenehen yelled: 'I've killed him! I've killed him!' He was happy. For a second he was boundlessly happy. Until he saw the blood on his hands, and then he felt ill.

II

I, Werner Friedrich Hartung, was born in this city on 20 August 1917. I attended university here, studied German and graduated with a dissertation on verbal expressions of the Absolute.

Afflicted from childhood with a lame foot, I was not called up into the army. For four years I taught German, and also art history and Latin. In the end I was teaching a graduating class. Because of the times, relations with my pupils were rather tense. I think they despised me. In their eyes I was not a patriot.

My wife's name was Elfriede. My son was called after his grandfathers: Sebastian and Robert. We lived in the north of the city. It was a four-room apartment. One of the rooms belonged to my little son.

I had painted his bed, the wardrobe and the other furniture all pink. The rocking-horse was covered with real hide. On the walls there were pictures from fairy-tales – Hansel and Gretel, Little Red-Riding-Hood and the wolf.

I often played with my son in that room. There were trees under the window. I was always happy there.

They came in battle formation; the first wave. Swarms of locusts with human intelligence. Four miles up they crept through the air. Bomber next to bomber, wings almost touching. They flashed in the sun. When the lieutenant held his hand against the light, he saw the fighters, too. Insects above the squadron, buzzing through the clouds. The planes' propellers drove the wind ahead of them, he could feel it in his face. The floor beneath his feet began to shake. His prosthesis chafed against the stump of his arm. His old wound stung. There was nothing he could do about it. He had no time, he was already surrounded by the roar of the engines. He shouted: 'Open fire!'

Eight gunners pulled back their cords. Lightning flashed through the position. A gust of pressure swept the charred earth. An impact winded him, and at the same time the salvo ripped into the sky.

He sensed straight away that there were only seven shells.

Only when everything had passed, the jet of flame before his eyes, the smoke, did he see the ragged muzzle, the ruined gun-mount. And the corpses: three gunners, six schoolboys. The head of the class was still alive. Blood-drenched, he writhed on the floor. His arms pointed backwards. Intestines spilled out. He was last in the class this time. Before he could even die, the bombs came.

The lieutenant tried to shout something. The blast slammed his mouth shut. He thought: not like the head of class!

But the explosions lifted him up and hurled him to the ground. He pressed himself into the earth but the shock-waves picked him up again. He thought: I'm breaking apart. He didn't break apart.

Something clenched at his throat. He thought: I'm suffocating. He didn't suffocate. A fist struck his lungs. Everything was threatening to explode. He felt nothing more.

'Let me out now,' said the man in civvies. He leaned against the wall. His breath was hoarse. A torch-beam fell on his face.

The wireless operator aimed the torch at the loudspeaker. 'Carpet-bombing on the position. Be glad we're alive.'

He lifted the receiver.

'I've got to get out!' the man explained distractedly. 'My child is at the station.'

The wireless operator announced into the mouthpiece: 'Bertha Three here!' He turned around. 'As a teacher you belong with your class.'

He put the torch down on the table. The beam fell against the ceiling.

'Let me out!'

A voice came from the receiver.

'Bertha Three, why aren't you firing! The order was: barrage!'

'Enemy activity over Bertha Three,' replied the operator.

'Wait till you've given your report!'

Behind his back the man tried the handle and rattled at the door.

'Stop that nonsense,' said the operator. 'When the lieutenant gets back you can talk to him.'

He went on listening to the voice in the receiver.

'The lieutenant could be dead or wounded.'

'Then someone else will come.'

The voice in the radio asked: 'Bertha Three, what's happening with your report?'

'My radio communication's gone! Wait a moment!'

While the operator was talking, he aimed the torch at the door-handle. The man's hand was in the beam. He gave a reply that the operator could not understand.

The voice on the wireless shouted: 'I need your report!'

'Just wait another minute!'

The man replied: 'It's quiet outside now.'

'Don't you feel the ground shaking?' The operator looked at the floor.

'It's coming from the station!' The man's voice turned shrill. 'My wife and child!'

'There's nothing you can do for them!'

The voice from the wireless said: 'Bertha Three, I can't make out a word!'

The operator shone the torch-beam into the man's face. 'And he isn't talking to you, either.'

The voice in the receiver said: 'Order from the commander! Go straight away and see what's going on in your position.'

'I'm going. Bertha Three, loud and clear!' The operator

dropped the receiver in its cradle and reached into his pocket for the key. He leapt to the door and unlocked it. Daylight dazzled his eyes.

The man pushed him aside. 'At last,' he groaned. He dashed up the stairs in front of the wireless operator and disappeared.

The girl pulled open the door to the air-raid cellar, and the candle went out. She stumbled in through the darkness. A man's voice said: 'That was my foot.'

She hadn't felt anything. A drop of sweat ran over her lips. It tasted salty. Maybe the house will burn down, she thought, then it will be a secret.

'Shut the door!' someone called from the wall.

Footsteps rang on the tiles. Someone was trying to get to the door.

She said hastily: 'There's the widow from the fourth floor still to come.' But the door was already shut. It was the man with the stiff leg. His foot dragged across the floor.

'What widow?'

People were moving. There was a hubbub of whispers by the wall. She couldn't make out a word, until someone finally said: 'We never know our neighbours as well as we should.'

The darkness remained. The threads of a cobweb dangled from the ceiling and brushed against her forehead. Her hand touched a body. Something fell to the floor. Matches.

'Careful!'

'Sorry!' Breath struck her face. There was a musty smell, it came from the walls. The cellar was damp.

'Did you turn off the gas tap?' asked a feeble voice.

'There's no gas left.'

Another voice asked slyly: 'Miss, wasn't that you carrying the sick woman down the stairs?'

She didn't reply. Her heart was beating too loudly. She put her hands to her chest. Into the silence someone said: 'It's starting!'

A faint rumble came through the wall. She felt a touch at her shoe. The man was still looking for the matches. The sly voice began again: 'Is she still up there?' The voice was insistent. Someone who wanted to get to the bottom of something.

Wood creaked. A bench was being shifted near the wall. The man on the floor started panting. Suddenly heavy thuds came from outside. The cellar fell silent. Even the breathing at her feet.

'It's just flak.'

'We've never heard it as loud as that before.'

Light flickered up. From the wall six faces stared into the match-flame. They sat motionless, statues arranged along a wall.

'Thank God,' said the man. 'That took a long time.'

A listless voice said: 'Time passes slower in the dark.'

The beams supporting the vault loomed out of the darkness. The girl hid her head in the gloom behind them. She could just make out the feet of the bench. The man held the match to a candle, and the booming noise from outside came closer.

'There she is!' someone called in surprise. The voice that had been asking about the widow.

The girl turned slowly, and the other woman stood motionless by the door. They looked into each other's eyes, but the man came and stood between them with the candle, making it impossible for them to come up with a story.

'So you left her up there?' It was always the same one who seemed so interested. She had a cardboard box containing a gas-mask between her feet.

'If you ask me,' an old person's voice began from the corner, 'no one could carry such a heavy person downstairs.'

'Quite right, Fredi!'

The girl looked across. An old man's hand was illuminated. It held a pipe.

'And no one would expect you to.'

A faint tremble ran across the floor. The rumble behind the wall became more distinct. Now it was coming out of the vault as well. The man walked over to the wall.

'Only two minutes,' a voice came reassuringly. 'Then it'll be over.'

'I hope so!'

Fear spread. The girl clutched the beam. She said: 'I didn't mean to.'

Six faces immediately stared over at her. The widow by the door pressed her hand to her mouth. She suppressed a cry. 'Come over to me,' the old man in the corner said, putting his pipe in his pocket. He looked at the vault. The girl didn't know who he was talking to. Somewhere something hissed. It grew louder. 'Get away from the door!'

'Here, beside me!' a woman volunteered. Her hand pointed to the bench. The widow came hesitantly over from the doorway. The hissing noise had faded away. Hard blows shook the walls. They were getting closer, rhythmic, like inter-mittent bursts of drum rolls.

Someone whispered: 'Wet your handkerchief.'

The girl pressed herself to the wood. In the corner the old man didn't say anything more.

'Wet your handkerchief.'

One of the six people sitting on the bench bent over the bowl. Her hand went into the water. She quickly drew it back. Drops fell on the stones. Suddenly wailing sounds filled the air. Sand trickled from the ceiling. Voices began to weep.

'No!' Immediately the women fell silent again. The wails grew louder, mingled with a whistling noise. The girl began whimpering quietly. The walls moved. A blast lashed the floor. The wind from the blast rushed in and extinguished the candles. The beam slipped away and the girl stumbled against the wall. Fingers clawed at her shoulder. Something swept down from the ceiling, and all of a sudden there was silence.

'Is anyone hurt?'

No one answered. They all began panting violently. There was dust in the darkness. It threatened to choke them.

'I'm going to put some light on!' The man moved. The crashing was still there, but further away. Only when the candle was lit did they start moving. The girl saw shadows. Mortar was crumbling to the floor. The man hobbled to the door as though through a curtain. Metal clanked. 'It's jammed!'

Outlines emerged as the light grew clearer. 'Can anyone help?' asked the man. 'The door won't open.' A cry rang out, and heads on the bench turned with a jerk. The girl, too, looked into the corner where the old man had been sitting. The first thing she could make out was the hand and the pipe. They were sticking out from under the beam.

'Herr Rainer!' The man was acting as though he was trying to wake him up. 'Herr Rainer!'

A woman said: 'The beam! The beam has killed him.'

'No!'

The voice that wanted to know everything declared: 'Of course it has!'

A sob started up beside the dead man. 'Fredi!' The voice whimpered. 'My dearest little Fredi!'

At that the widow began to giggle.

'Young lady!' ordered the man.

The girl sat up. She felt her way over a suitcase to the door. Behind her the voice whimpered: 'Fredi, stay with me.' The man grasped the bolt, but the door suddenly opened of its own accord. Stones clattered down. The man turned around. He spread his arms as though making an announcement. He spoke: 'We're buried alive!'

The squadrons dropped their bombs before they reached the flak tower. The gun commander saw them coming. The dots dropping from the planes grew bigger and slanted towards him. In swarms, like stones from slingshots, dense as a steel mesh, just missing the smooth platform. The wailing they made was unbearable. They disappeared half a mile off into the houses beyond the tower in smoke and cascades of rubble. Shock waves pulsed outwards, sweeping across the roofs. Embers sailed through the air. A factory chimney toppled half the width of a street, bent in the middle, then burst apart. The district disappeared behind a pall of thick smoke.

'Fighter from the right!' shouted the loader. He lay on his belly and turned his head. They jumped up and became a machine. 'Fall in,' ordered the gun commander. They didn't hear a word, and yet they did as he asked. The four barrels turned to the side. The gunners dangled from the base of the gun on their straps. What the gun did, they did too.

'Ammunition!' The gun commander turned the sights and the fighter came closer.

'A hundred and twenty rounds!' shouted the loader. 'Ready!'

The gun commander bit his lip, pulled the trigger. He was half-blinded by flames, but the fighter hung in his cross-hairs. The gun shook feverishly. He was deafened by the explosions. Not a single shot reached the fighter. The plane was too far away. Behind the graveyard it disappeared into a wall of soot.

'Load!'

The gun commander thought: I'm just issuing commands for my own sake. He shouted: 'He's coming back!'

When the loader tore open the basket, the empty cartridge cases fell on to the concrete. No one heard them. Amidst the crashing of the bombs, no one could have heard the collapsing buildings or the sound of a human voice. The air was filled with roaring.

The lieutenant opened his eyes. His lids stuck together. Everything blurred. A face, eyes, a row of teeth. There was a gaping hole in the middle. He saw lips moving, but heard nothing. Something inside him was broken, he didn't know what. He hovered in mid-air, somewhere between earth and sky. Light as a feather. First he must get back. The battery position swayed before his eyes. Gun-barrels swung. He tried to blink. He had a sense that the air was crammed with noise.

The wireless operator began to sit him up, reaching for his good hand. He said: 'I've got headquarters on the phone!'

'Why can't you speak up?' There was a burning pain in his chest. The operator held out his arm to him. He made an effort to support himself on it. He got to his feet. When he touched his face he felt something warm. He thought: blood. He wiped his hand over his chin, then looked at his hand. Nothing but spittle.

'I've got headquarters on the phone!' shouted the wireless operator.

'I hear you!' He thought: I've gone deaf. That's all I need.

He suddenly looked into the emplacement. Two guns lay abandoned there. He asked confusedly: 'Where are the gunners?'

'In the dug-outs, lieutenant.'

'I can't make out a word.'

'They've run away!' shouted the operator. He pointed to the ground with his finger. 'Dug-outs!' Pointlessly, he looked at the lieutenant's mouth. Something whooshed past behind him. They both ducked mechanically, but the bomb had already gone by. It exploded a hundred yards away in the lawn behind them. Earth sprayed into the sky, and smoke flickered like a torch. Startled, the lieutenant thought: I can't hear a thing. It's just as though I'd gone blind.

'Anti-aircraft fire!' shouted the radioman. 'Headquarters wants anti-aircraft fire!'

'All right!' He nodded. 'Tell them we're going to fire again in three minutes.' He turned around. Behind him the wireless operator started moving. The head of the class lay in front of him. To get to the dug-outs he had to go past him. Past a mass of flesh and blood. One leg lay askew over his ribcage. His head was missing a chin. He closed his eyes. He thought:

His mother will be here in two hours. He stumbled away across the charred earth.

'Stop,' a voice gasped.

The girl leaned against the wall and stared into the corner. The candle lit her face. Wetness ran over her thighs, ran over her calves on to the tiles. She was standing in a puddle. For a moment she was more ashamed than afraid, but no one was looking at her feet.

'Pray,' someone suggested.

The vault went on groaning. The dull noise behind the walls rose and faded away again. The girl felt movement behind her. She bit her lips. Everything was furred, as though it was rotten already.

'She's tearing his arm off,' a voice screeched. In the corner the old woman was pulling at the corpse. She was battling with the wooden beam, which resisted her frenzy. What she was doing was pointless. She couldn't get more than the arm out. The beam was jammed.

'Silence!' ordered the man.

No one obeyed. The girl thought: Neither will I.

Then she felt ashamed. She suddenly beat her chest with her fists. 'I don't want to die,' she shouted.

III

I, Alfred Rainer, known to my wife as Fredi, was born in this city on 9 March 1871. We had a garden behind the graveyard. I had built an arbour and planted tobacco, and in fine weather we sat in the sun. My wife knitted. When evening came we went home. I don't want to remember my youth. You forget the bad parts, and the good parts were too rare. I was a member of the choral society and the animal protection league. We used to have a dog. But we were always a bit lonely. With the passing of the years we had got used to it. You can argue about happiness. I didn't work that out until later.

In the event of my demise, I would like the choral society to sing the soldiers' chorus from 'Margarete', and I would like to be cremated. On 2 July 1944, between one and two in the afternoon, I died. My death was probably pointless. It harmed no one and benefited no one, but I make no complaint about that.

Anyone still whimpering was silenced. Anyone still shouting shouted in vain. Technology shattered technology. It bent masts, tore apart machines, opened up craters, demolished walls, and life was just so much rubbish. Twelve-year-old human flesh slammed into the door of the bunker. The flesh was held together by a belt.

The boy drummed against the door with his fists. He roared: 'Open up!'

The iron stayed mute. Hair hung over the boy's forehead. Only when blood was running over his hands did he spot the handle. Seconds passed before the door opened a chink. It seemed like hours to him. He leapt through the gap like an animal. He was in flight, and staggered against the concrete walls.

'Next door,' a voice said.

Great crevices gaped open. He stepped through the middle of a wall. He thought: I'm saved. He put his hand to his helmet. 'Report from the station! The big air-raid shelter has taken a direct hit!'

'Go on,' a voice ordered.

'We need a rescue party!' He couldn't say more than that. Suddenly the voices rang in his ears. Ninety children, two hundred women, sixty-four men. Writhing under shattered concrete slabs, a single scream of horror. The boy's face began to contort. His vocal cords babbled. When a hand closed his mouth he sank to the ground. Shadows crowded in on him. A man asked: 'What's his name? I'll have to jot it down. The boy should get a medal!' But he didn't hear that. Nonsensically, all he heard was the exclamation: 'Of course he does, he's earned one!'

A house collapsed. The three-storey facade folded up on itself. Six sets of furnishings, along with ovens, bath-tubs and lavatory bowls, fell onto the cellar. The courtyard became a rubbish dump. Ashes and smoke flew into the sky. The shock waves from the next bombs churned up the debris. Air pressure swept what was in the air fifty yards down the street. Air twisted an iron joist into a spiral. Air reduced a vault to ruins, and heat set light to anything flammable as though it were celluloid.

Linoleum, internal doors and bread in a tin box. The ceiling of a utility room split apart as though made of porcelain. The shock wave from an air-mine lifted the lot into the air. When the lieutenant saw it in the distance, it looked like a volcano erupting.

He tore open the door of the dug-out. The gunners crouched in the darkness.

'Get out!'

An eternity passed. He couldn't recognise them. The noise at his back was unbearable. The worst thing was that he could only feel it. He was still deaf.

'Get out!'

He listened into the darkness. There was no echo. When still no one moved, he tried to use reason.

'Comrades, at this time everyone must do his duty.'

He looked at his leather hand. Rage welled up in him. He was a cripple urging them to share his fate. 'Is there no one here,' he asked, 'with a mother out there?' He was disgusted. 'A sister or a brother!' He couldn't tell whether he was shouting or whispering. He said: 'Think of your mothers!'

One of them stood up.

The boy stepped out of the darkness into the light. His uniform exposed the gauntness of his body. He was volunteering not out of heroism, but out of habit.

The lieutenant roared: 'Next!'

Again seconds passed. No one stood up. He reached for his belt. As he unbuckled it, he recognised their faces. Huddled together, they cowered on the ground like animals. He lifted his arm, quite slowly. Then, quick as lightning, he tore into them. Only when the belt buckle smacked against their helmets did they leap to their feet. They pushed their way to the door. With careless blows he drove them up the steps. He rained blow after blow on their backs. They ran panting from him. Sweat ran down their faces. He stared after them.

They were flying through cloud. The engines roared. Rain drummed against the windscreens. Fog or steam. It passed by outside like the white walls of a tunnel. The sounds didn't change. The vibration of the frame, the tick of the instruments and the humming of the wind.

The wireless operator came forward to Captain Lester and handed him a piece of paper.

Mission accomplished. Squadron dismissed. Bon voyage!

Captain Lester looked up, and his eyes froze. He couldn't move. His pulse missed a beat. His feet grew lifeless. By the time his brain was working again it was already too late.

The port propeller of the plane next to them sawed through the wing; it emerged from the gloom and sheared its way through the metal from behind like a drill-bit. Shavings rattled against the nose. Fuel sprayed, like a banner. The second pilot hurled his body against the elevator control. A quake ran through the bomber. The wing was amputated.

Captain Lester leapt from his seat. That was the signal. Emergency doors suddenly flew into the void. Figures tore at straps. They braced themselves in the airflow, staggered from their seats; a moment later they were in the air. Strenehen saw them disappearing. A scream welled from his mouth. His turret panel wouldn't open. He beat his fist against the catch. It was like striking an anvil. He hurled himself against the struts. The effort made blood run to his head. By the time he tried to force his way through the shattered glass, the plane was already plummeting. Then he gave up. He hurled himself down through the shaft on to the flight deck. When he hit the bomb racks he dislocated his arm. Pain coursed through him like a great flame. Ohm's face was before his eyes for a second, then he saw the sky and staggered towards it. Through the port-side opening, with an arm outstretched – like a wounded bird – he fell.

Into an infinite depth. Towards the earth.

The man was running mechanically. He had forgotten that one of his legs was too short. One whole step and two halves.

Keep going. He ran through the graveyard. Sun warmed his back. A tree lay in his path.

He jumped through the branches. He didn't feel the blow to his forehead, because he was thinking: My child.

His lungs heaved. Splinters whirred against a gravestone. Never mind. He had to go on. He thought: My child.

Something white loomed up. Whistling noises sliced the air.

A war memorial column. A roaring noise came from the sky. The column tipped over.

Always two half-steps and one whole step.

Onwards.

Flowers whirled through the air. Fell at his feet. He jumped over paths as though over hurdles. He thought: my child. The graveyard was endless. A crater gaped in the ground. He fell into it and landed on a board. The wood was worm-eaten. With rotten flesh smeared on his fingers, he climbed out again without thinking. He dashed on. My child!

Rows of graves – the station – burial urns – at the far end – family graves – the path – urns!

It was seven hundred yards to the first houses. He panted his way past generations of corpses. The limping father.

He sweated, panted, ran. One whole step. Two halves. He headed onwards.

My child!

Air rushed through the window, yanking up the curtains. The curtain-rods shot from their hooks and everything fell to the floor. The tablecloth billowed. The playing-cards scattered. Herr Cheovski stood up. 'What's the point of it all? We'll be dead in five minutes.'

'United,' replied his wife. She looked raptly into his face. He envied his wife her faith. The sideboard door opened. Wineglasses toppled over, smashed on to the parquet, burst into a hundred splinters.

'Come to the wall!'

Herr Cheovski walked over to her and held out his arm. Their hands touched shyly. For a moment she pressed his fingers firmly, then he guided her slowly towards the door. He saw the room, the open window. Smoke swirled across the floor. The floor was coated with dust. His patent shoes had left tracks. Footprints like an animal's led from the table to him. He thought how pointless it was that someone had bothered to fit the parquet slats together. Hard work, he thought. I wonder if the man is still alive. The pendulum of the grandfather clock swung as though in fog. It was eleven minutes past one.

Sergeant Jonathan Strenehen, twenty-four years old, the son of a man who enjoyed a glass of beer with his lunch, was falling at an acceleration rate of thirty-two feet per second per second. He fell with his belly to the sun and his back to the earth.

His dislocated arm blew against his body. Three hundred feet down it jammed itself between his legs. Air pressure clamped them together like a vice. Man, material, leather fell vertically according to the law of gravity. The earth's crust hurtled towards him like a concrete wall. It came with the speed of a bullet. His brain tried to register it. During those seconds he did not remember his birth, first communion, a girl he imagined he loved. He loved himself most of all. There were no images of the past, no thoughts of the future. There was just a body flying through the air.

His primitive brain, his cerebrum, activated his nerves. It gave him a consciousness of fear that increased by the yard. He calculated in advance what would happen. The first contact. His spine on the stone surface, nearly three miles below. The impact of the back of his head. The cracks in his skull. The immediate shattering of the pelvis. The splintering of the elbows. Fear worked precisely, like an automaton. Meanwhile his higher brain, his cerebellum, concerned itself with thought. With moving the muscles of his right arm as it tried and failed to pull the ripcord of a parachute that would not open. It could not do so, because of his dislocated shoulder-blade. That pause saved the life of Sergeant Jonathan Strenehen, the son of a woman who thought of him twenty-four hours out of twenty-four. The two-row thousand-horsepower radial engine with the three-blade propeller missed him by two and a half feet as it sped past, and missed the still unopened parachute. The air pressure pushed Strenehen six feet sideways. A wave of heat enveloped him.

By the time the parachute opened with a jolt, Strenehen had flown nine hundred yards through the air. His left hand had managed the grip that his right refused to perform. The jolt brought his body from a fall to a glide. Sergeant Jonathan Strenehen hovered. In that moment he thought with uncanny force about his mother.

In the air-lock of the bunker six men and four women reached for shovels, put on their helmets, pulled the straps over their chins. They stood in a semicircle like soldiers. But they weren't soldiers.

'We'll walk in single file,' their leader said. 'Fifteen feet apart.' He took some military blankets out of a barrel of water and handed them out. The ground grew damp with moisture. The thudding of the bombs came from outside. A fan drove air into their faces. Someone began to cough. It sounded hollow. They draped the wet blankets round their shoulders. Steam rose. Something hummed on and on – the fan over the door and the fan in the wall.

'You stay there,' the leader ordered and pointed at a boy. The boy's chin was scattered with pimples, and he had red hair.

'Why?' he asked, insulted.

He wore a band on his arm. It was rolled up. No one could read what it said.

'Because!' replied the leader of the troop. He fell silent and then continued: 'You take command of the air-lock.'

His eye fell on the others, but they looked through him. He knew what they were thinking.

'Do we need buckets?' asked a woman.

'No, no buckets,' the women beside her replied. One of the men looked for his watch. When he took it out, they all looked at its hands. First one after another, then all together. The leader of the troop picked up a blanket as well. The watch flashed silver. The big hand and the little hand pointed at numbers. Nobody saw them. Neither the numbers nor the hands. They stared at the watch. There was no reason to wait any longer.

'Who wants to be last? I'll take the lead!'

The troop leader deliberately did not look at the men. 'Me!' a voice announced. The voice was clear. Someone pushed his way forwards. The man wore a habit. Rosary beads dangled at his hip. It was a priest.

The troop leader studied his shoes. 'Don't strain yourself. No one's going to be praying over there!'

The shoes had high sides and laces, and looked like old women's shoes. They were standing in water.

'Who said anything about praying?' The priest pulled a pick-axe out of the boy's hands and joined the men. He stepped from one puddle into the next. His fingernails were rimmed with black.

'Are you doing it for God?'

'If you want to talk to me about God, come to my church when the war's over. It's burnt down, but I'm going to build it up again.'

'You hope!' The troop leader suddenly spat at the wall.

'Let's go!' He turned around. In passing a woman ran her hand over the head of the red-haired boy. She was a year older and his sister.

They lay on the platform, and their fingernails clawed into the concrete. The straps were tense – their connection with the earth.

'Fire!' roared the gun commander. He pointed one arm to the horizon. A flame licked in a cloud. It sprayed apart in the shape of a comet. Lightning flashed. At the same time a blow shook the whole flak tower. The commander drew in his arm at once and huddled against the ground. The concrete radiated warmth. He didn't notice. The air hissed like steam. Stones and earth sprayed up from the street and vanished into the sky. The lid of an ammunition box sprang back. The blast tore it from its hinges. It slipped off and skimmed across the platform like a projectile, towards the loader.

Who screamed.

The commander didn't hear it, but he saw it: the loader's face. A face filled with fear. When the lid smashed into it, the commander closed his eyes. A second later the blast lifted him high and flung him onto his back.

The gun commander slid, arms outstretched, towards the loader. The concrete ripped skin from his hands. His rope slipped on to his chest. While the noose held him, something broke in his hip. The pain ran through his body like a stab from a dagger.

'Hold on!' he shouted. 'Hold on!'

He meant the ropes. If the ropes failed, he would plummet into the abyss, four storeys below. For the gun commander at that moment the bare concrete was a symbol of life.

Receiver jammed between shoulder and chin, the wireless operator was smoking a cigarette. The light flickered again. The door stood open a crack. Outside they were shouting orders. He blew a cloud of smoke up to the ceiling. Drops of water hung from the concrete.

From the receiver came the sound of someone clearing his throat. 'Bomber stream, two thousand feet wide, twenty miles long.'

A voice from the far distance ordered: 'Break it up!'

'Get off the line,' said a woman's voice. The wireless operator drew on his cigarette. A gold ring flashed on his finger. It reminded him of his wife. He pushed the cigarette into the corner of his mouth.

'Am I through to Bertha Central or not?'

'Bertha Central here,' came a voice in his ear.

He replied: 'Bertha Three speaking. Note: third gun out

due to burst barrel. Losses: one NCO, two corporals; six anti-aircraft auxiliaries. Resuming fire in a minute. Over!'

A whistle came through the receiver. The voice asked: 'Shall I repeat?'

'No!' The operator looked through the crack of the door at the sky. The bombers were flying in a V-formation like wild ducks. Above the gun emplacement they turned southwards. He asked: 'Anything else?'

'Yes!'

He looked at the dots. He could not imagine that people were sitting in them. His thoughts jumbled together.

'Are you still there?'

'Yes!'

'Enemy plane down in map quadrant four. The crew baled out. They're still in the air. Bertha Three is to muster a unit to deal with the crew. The parachutes are drifting into your zone. Over! Do you read me?'

A quake ran across the ground. The door banged shut. In the emplacement they fired the first salvoes.

'Right now?' asked the operator.

The voice replied: 'When did you think?'

'Who issued the order for the unit?'

'The commander.'

'Yes sir!' The operator repeated: 'Enemy plane crash, map quadrant four. Crew bailed out. Bertha Three to muster a squad to take them prisoner.'

'Not word-perfect, but I'm not pedantic, it was broadly correct. What's your name?'

The wireless operator answered: 'Lance Corporal Weigand!'

'Hello, Weigand!'

The man at the end of the line hung up. There was a
crackle in the operator's receiver. The cigarette slipped from
his mouth. It fell on to his trousers. He snatched at it, and it
dived into the leg of his right boot. Cursing, he leapt to his
feet.

IV

I, Nikolai Petrovich, was born on New Year's Day 1903 in Krivoy Rog on the river Bug. I was an engineer on a tug working between Saratov and Astrakhan. My log cabin stood on the shore in Rastonia. Every year at Easter we slaughtered a lamb. We were full and happy. There were thirty thousand of us in the camp in Minsk. We threw our dead naked into the pits. Each one held a hundred starved bodies. If they were just children, proportionally more. We had special pits for them. If you layer children and adults on top of each other you get gaps. Space in the pits was very tight. I didn't count the pits. There were so many pits on the stretch between Minsk and this city.

I expect my wife Lisaveta is dead. I expect little Lisaveta is dead too. I expect little Andrei Nikolaevich is dead; my son. At night I dream about bread. Dry bread, over and over again. Bread.

It sounded as though they were aboard a ship. The vaulted ceiling creaked, and so did the floor and the walls. A machine throbbed behind them.

The widow asked: 'Can't you be quiet?'

The old woman squatted by the dead man in the corner and sobbed. The beam hid the corpse, but she stroked the protruding hand.

'Air,' said a woman. 'What about air?'

The candle flame grew smaller. It guttered. The girl stared into it with glazed eyes. Only her lips moved. The flame was reflected in her pupils. The girl was lying on the tiles with her arms outstretched.

The woman spoke again. 'We've got to save air!'

Two arms came out of the darkness, searched for the box on the floor. The hands pulled the gas-mask out of the box, carefully, as though it was forbidden. Silently hands and mask vanished again into the darkness. The sobbing of the old women and the pulsing beats behind the walls remained the only sound.

'Where are the shovels?' asked the man.

'What for?' The voice came from the bench. Someone's foot bumped against the bowl. It rang out clearly.

'We've got to dig ourselves out!'

'There'll be no digging here,' said the widow. 'If we move, the vault will collapse.'

The man yelled suddenly: 'Do you want to suffocate?'

They all listened for a moment. Even the old woman in the corner. They looked fearfully upwards. But the vault was stronger than the echo. The voice rebounded loudly, but nothing moved.

All at once the old woman began. 'His last words were: take care of my wife!' She lifted the dead man's arm and showed it to the others. The skin was stretched over the fingers. Chalk-dust covered it like powder.

'I never heard that,' said the widow.

'You did, you did!'

'"My love!"' The widow laughed loudly, her face contorted. She struck her knee with her hand.

The man said menacingly: 'Will you be quiet!'

'I can't . . .' The widow broke off. New sounds began behind the walls. A drum-roll, still far off, started coming closer. It was moving slowly. Or at breakneck speed, they couldn't tell.

The wind drove Sergeant Strenehen towards the curtain of flak. Thirty-six guns were pouring twice that many shells into the sky every minute. They rose like rockets. He drifted helplessly onwards.

He thought: if they are human beings, they'll stop now.

In reply, thirty-six guns flashed on the ground below. A spray of fire. Shrapnel flew through the air at him. He drifted five hundred yards from the barrage. The first splinters whirred towards him. Some of them whistled.

He thought: perhaps they can't see me.

Of course they must have seen him, but he calculated the interval between an order being issued and its implementation. From observation point to headquarters, from headquarters to the guns.

There was a gap of thirty seconds between salvoes. He didn't know that, but he started counting. Two numbers made one second. At first he counted more slowly. Then faster. The straps of his parachute constricted his chest. Something was wrong. He could feel the pain in his shoulder joint. His dislocated arm grew as heavy as lead. When he had counted to twenty, fire flashed on the ground again. Two, three, four. An impact tore at his parachute. Strenehen closed his eyes and waited to fall. But it was only a shock wave. The explosions began to swing him from side to side. Twenty feet to the right, twenty feet to the left. He forced himself to count again. At the count of five a sudden gust came and forced the parachute sideways, dragging him with it. A mile up he suddenly found himself in a storm. A whirlwind spun him around. The parachute collapsed on itself and billowed up again.

He fell three hundred yards in an air pocket, then updraughts lifted him again. When the next salvo came he was more than half a mile away from the barrage. When he was driven sideways he wondered where the storm was coming from. Then it occurred to him that the city was on fire. It was only the beginning. Twenty minutes later the storm became a hurricane.

The trees lay on the paths in the graveyard. Burnt shrubs projected from a layer of haze. Smoke swirled over the graves.

There was a smell of dust. Nikolai Petrovich knew that. He was sitting in a narrow trench, with the others crouched beside him. Rastyeva was holding a board over his head. It was part of a coffin lid. Rastyeva looked like a dead man. If the bombs spared him, he would die of exhaustion.

Chikin was chewing on a leather strap. His hunger was greater than his fear.

When a cascade of stones rattled down, they ducked to the ground. Their guard had abandoned them. The trench was too pitiful. But it was good enough for them. When the next wave of carpet-bombing came, they would die, or else they wouldn't. Before it came, they struck a deal.

'If Rastyeva dies, I'm having his coat,' declared Nikolai.

'Your own jacket's perfectly good!'

Chikin didn't take the strap out of his mouth as he spoke. Spittle bubbled between his teeth. He was developing blisters. The strap was tough.

'And your jacket's even better.'

'Fine!' spat Chikin. 'Then I'll take his shoes!'

Nikolai Petrovich grabbed Rastyeva's shoulder. He shook him.

'Show us your shoes!'

Rastyeva lowered the board and raised one foot. It was wrapped in a sack. Knotted laces held it together. It was stiff with dirt.

'Where are your shoes?'

A flak splinter whirred through the air. It flew like a boomerang. At the edge of the trench it clattered into the ground. Earth sprayed up. There was a clank. Metal against stone.

'Look out!' shouted Chikin. He threw himself flat in the

ditch. As he fell, he grabbed for Rastyeva. There was no explosion.

'Stand up again,' said Nikolai. He turned to Rastyeva. 'Where are your shoes?'

'Bread,' whispered Rastyeva.

His beard was matted. Veins lay beneath the waxy skin as though under glass. He raised his hand and gestured listlessly. Fleshless bones stretched towards the sky. Chikin said: 'He swapped them for bread.'

'Where have you put the bread?'

Chikin took the strap out of his mouth. 'He ate all day yesterday.'

'What?'

Chikin shoved the strap back into his mouth. 'Crusts!' he said. 'Such crusts!' He showed their size between thumb and index finger.

'He didn't tell me!'

'I thought he'd have saved some,' said Chikin.

Nikolai spat into the ditch. 'He's eating everything we've got!'

'Not for long.' Chikin pushed the strap from one corner of his mouth into the other. The spittle ran into his lap. A long thread of mucus.

'Still,' said Nikolai, 'I'm having the coat!' The engine noise grew louder. He looked into the sky.

Chikin scratched his head with his right hand. 'Perhaps he's still got the crusts. We could share them between us.'

'Have a look in his pockets.'

'Not now. There's too many of us here, no one would get a thing.'

Chikin took the strap out of his mouth and licked it. The leather looked like a piece of intestine.

'Have you still got the crusts?' asked Nikolai. He spoke quietly. He looked suspiciously to the side, but the others cowered fifteen feet away from them.

'No!' Rastyeva shook his head.

'He's lying.'

'Give them to us of your own free will.'

Chikin whispered: 'I've eaten them.'

'You bastard!'

The howling of the bombs started up again. Nikolai Petrovich grabbed the piece of coffin-lid from Rastyeva and held it over his own head.

Anyone found looting will be shot! The man read it on a poster. He was standing in the entrance hall of the first apartment block he came to, and staring at the wall. The noise of the bombs echoed through the corridor. He had decided to wait. He thought: It's best for my child.

He was panting. Sunbeams fell on his shoes, but he was standing in the shade; the light came from outside.

A second passed. Nothing happened. Time seemed to creep.

Anyone found looting will be shot! He read it again. The poster was torn. A piece of plaster was missing from the wall. It lay on the ground.

Another second passed. The sunbeams at his feet grew brighter. The thick smoke drifted in the street. A fly buzzed in the hallway. He wondered where the fly had come from, and listened intently. He thought: If I get hit I won't be able to help my child. It was strange, but he didn't think about his wife.

Suddenly a voice asked: 'What are you doing here?'

Startled, he turned around. A soldier stood at the entrance to the stairwell. He held a gun under his arm, his hand on the trigger. There was a chain around his neck, and on the chain there was a metal tag.

The man said: 'Wait a moment!' He looked at the gun and saw the muzzle. It was just a hole. The rumble of engines sounded in the sky. Beyond the graveyard the guns rang out. He waited for the soldier to turn around and disappear. He started to laugh in embarrassment. He felt as though he were going to scream.

'Come here!' ordered the soldier. The gun was at his hip. The sights and muzzle formed a straight line. The fly buzzed towards him. He struck it aside with his left hand. There was mortar dust on his uniform.

'I've got to keep going,' said the man.

'Where to?'

'The station.'

The soldier shook his head. 'Come here!'

It was exactly six paces. The man had no option but to obey. He hobbled forwards. Now he could feel his foot again. It was an embarrassment to him. Then it occurred to him: it had been six paces from the teacher's desk to the door. The whole class had stared at his feet. So did the soldier. He couldn't explain.

'There is absolutely no point,' he assured him, 'in you stopping me.'

'I'll be the judge of that,' said the soldier. 'You're coming to the cellar with me right now.'

He was about to turn around.

At that moment the man struck his gun aside. It fell out of the soldier's hands and clanked on the stones.

'What on earth are you doing?' asked the soldier, startled.

'I've got to get to the station!' The man tried to get away, but his adversary was faster. A punch landed on his shoulder. The man tripped over his foot. He fell on his knees. A shinbone hit the cobbles. Pain flared through him, and he immediately felt the muzzle in his back.

'Stand up!'

The man struggled to his feet. Something warm was trickling down his calf. He wanted to think. I've got to get to my child: that was all that occurred to him. He hobbled a few paces in front of the soldier with the gun at his back. The entrance to a dark stairwell opened up before him. He saw steps. An arrow pointed downwards. Before he went down he turned around again. He looked like a beaten animal.

'Please!'

'Keep walking!'

The soldier shook his head and looked at his chest. The metal tag on the chain had got twisted. He straightened it.

The fighter plane flitted like a shadow over the roofs and suddenly climbed steeply. Strenehen saw it. It was German. The plane disappeared in a cloud of soot and emerged again on the other side. It kept away from the bombers. It was flying aimlessly. Or looking for something in particular.

It flew in a loop and came towards Strenehen, a bird of prey that has spied its target.

Strenehen thought: this can't be happening. The diagonal outline of a fighter plane was heading straight towards him. His parachute billowed above him. He hung stiffly in the straps. His body dangled in the wind. The wind lifted his legs. He saw his own shoes. Blood stained the leather. Dark brown stripes.

The German held his course, coming from the front. Air whirled around the propeller. What does he want, thought Strenehen. The pain in his arm faded. He raised his head. Surely Strenehen was too far away from the line of bombers? A few small clouds of dust floated between him and the fighter. Inexorably the plane grew bigger. Behind the glass of the cockpit Strenehen could make out the silhouette of a person. He stared at the wings. That's where they'll come from, the bullets from the machine guns. He thought desperately: He won't fire.

At that moment flames licked from the nose.

'Bastard,' shouted Strenehen.

He closed his eyes. He felt the draught of air beneath his body. It came from the propeller. The plane was already flying away beneath him. Now his parachute would rip, and then he would fall far into the depths. Only when nothing happened did Strenehen open his eyes. It seemed impossible to grasp. At me, he thought, aggrieved. He was firing at me. He was enveloped in smoke. He floated through it. Again he heard the engine of the fighter. The plane circled above him, dipped. It floated past a hundred feet away. The pilot turned his head. He raised a threatening fist. The image flashed by. The plane turned away. Soon it was nothing but a slanting line. Strenehen couldn't follow its flight any more. The parachute blocked his view. He felt the pain in his arm again.

The road surface crackled like paper. The rescue party from the flak tower dashed along the street. They ran in single file, ten yards apart, the women between the men. The wet blankets flapped above their heads. The priest held his pick like a cross. He could feel his heart pounding. The storm drove ashes over the roadway. A crumpled car lay on the footpath. The air was filled with smoke. Broken glass covered the cobbles. A door was torn off. One by one they scurried between the wrecked chassis and the wall. The crater gaped behind the wreck. A twisted pipe stuck up. It came out of the earth. It was ragged at the tip. The priest ran past it. It made him think of gas, but he couldn't smell anything. The street narrowed to a gorge. He saw flames. They licked up from window frames, licked up to the sky. The rescue party disappeared beneath them as though into a tunnel. One after the other they leapt into the smoke.

The priest saw the hole beneath the flames in front of him. The chain around his neck slipped outside his habit. His little cross dangled at his chest. He tugged it off and stuck it in his pocket. He was the last. If he got hit, no one would notice. He thought: not even God. I'm too insignificant. Then he disappeared into the smoke.

Sparks sprayed over the platform. The gun commander knelt on one knee, unfolded the bandage and placed it on the loader's face. A gap yawned between brow and lips. Amidst raw flesh, bone gleamed. He asked: 'Aré you in pain?'

'No, I can't feel a thing.' The loader was about to put his hand to his face, but the gun commander stopped him. Shock waves hissed over the concrete. Dust enveloped them. He wrapped the bandage around his head.

'Am I going to die?' A little blood ran from the wounded man's mouth. Next to the ruin of his face it seemed harmless.

'Something like that wouldn't kill you!' The gun commander looked over to the others. They lay on the concrete and looked up. One of them crept to the gun. His helmet hung at the back of his neck. His strap no longer held him to his gun, but he clutched it tightly with his hands. The loader suddenly roared: 'My nose is gone!' It sounded like a joke. At once a gush of blood came from his mouth. The gunner with the strap in his hands had reached the gun and crept past him. He wanted to reach the edge of the platform. That was where the ladder was.

'I don't know anyone without a nose,' gurgled the loader. He wept. The tears mingled with the blood. He drove the blood from his mouth with his breath and asked persistently: 'What's wrong with my nose?'

'Nothing! It's bleeding, that's all!'

'Two holes instead of a nose!' The loader screamed. 'I know what that looks like!'

'Nonsense!' The gun commander looked at the gunner by the ladder. The boy was reaching for the rungs. Dropping his strap, he quickly glanced across.

The gun commander put the bandage down, stretched out an arm and waggled his index finger. Then the boy laid himself on his belly again and began to creep back. Inching along with his chin to the ground and his backside stuck up in the air, he looked like a dog waiting to be beaten.

'I can't feel anything at all,' the loader gurgled again.

'Sit still, or I can't put the bandage on you!'

The loader answered: 'Now I'm going to spend my whole life alone.'

He was already talking like someone planning his future.

'Don't speak!' The gun commander shook his head. 'You'll get the Wound Badge. Girls like that.'

'Without a nose!' roared the loader.

'But you've got your nose!'

The loader answered reproachfully: 'It's over there!' He pointed a hand towards the concrete. A piece of flesh lay on the platform. It was his nose.

V

Dear Mother,

Today, on my twentieth birthday, just a few lines. You really don't need to worry, but it's impossible for you to visit me. I have to train recruits to an anti-aircraft battery. I would have no time to see you, and I can't get time off. Of course I'm not yet ready to fight at the front. I still feel the wound when I breathe, but I think it's healed well. But I can't taste cigarettes any more. My father can have them all now. Have you had any news of him? The letter in March was the last I heard from him. I'm sure it's not serious. Sometimes post gets lost, or left somewhere. Believe me, I am sure my father is well, and please: stop consulting the stars. Lie down and go to sleep, my dear mother, that way we are always together in our thoughts. Now I must close again. My shift is beginning.

A thousand greetings and all love from your son.

P.S. No, we are not in the city, Mother. Do I have to keep repeating that? Mother!

There was a crash above the gun emplacement. The lieutenant shut the door and the sounds grew quieter. The smell of gunpowder clung to the walls. A sheet of smoke hovered above the floor.

The wireless operator shouted: 'You should put on a helmet, Lieutenant!'

'What are you shouting about?' The lieutenant looked at the table. 'Give me a cigarette!'

The operator opened his mouth. 'I thought . . .'

'Leave it!' the lieutenant said. 'I've got cigarettes of my own.' He reached into his pocket. Morse signals came from the set in the corner. They echoed through the bunker. The smoke on the floor congealed.

'Where's the teacher?'

'He cleared off.' The operator shook his head. 'He was desperate to get to the station.'

'He won't get there alive.'

'Nothing we can do about that.'

'No.' The lieutenant put a cigarette in his mouth. He lit a

match, and it went out again. It was like a laundry in the bunker now. Steamy and damp. He asked: 'Do you think it's right?'

'What?'

'Oh, nothing,' answered the lieutenant.

The operator lit a match. He held it out. With the cigarette in his mouth the lieutenant leaned over the table. The flame scorched the paper, and finally the tobacco burned. The lieutenant breathed out.

'I've got an order here,' said the operator. 'There's an enemy flight crew in the air.' He pointed to a piece of paper. It lay folded on the table.

'Issued on the phone?'

'Yes.'

The lieutenant took the piece of paper. His hand shook, and the writing blurred before his eyes. He glanced at the wall, looked into the mirror and started from the beginning again. Suddenly he threw the paper on the floor.

'Absolutely no question!' he shouted.

'It's an order.'

'An order I refuse to carry out. No one is leaving the position during the raid.'

'Yes, Lieutenant.'

'If someone dies *here* I can answer for it. Do you understand what I mean?'

'Yes.'

'Then wipe the dirt off your face.'

'Yes sir!' The wireless operator reached for his handkerchief. He blew his nose.

The lieutenant asked: 'Who issued that order anyway?'

'I asked the same question. It was the commanding officer.'

'The commanding officer?'

'They've made a note of my name. It isn't going to be easy for you.'

The lieutenant walked over to the mirror. 'You're an idiot.'

'What should I have done?'

'Hung up in the middle of the conversation!'

'I never thought of that.'

'Fine, then go upstairs now, choose a few people and send them off.'

'Me?' The operator's jaw dropped.

'Yes, you!'

The operator reached for the headphones behind his back. 'I can't leave here. You know that.'

'Of course!' The lieutenant laughed. 'Anything else?'

'Yes. A private call.'

The lieutenant raised his head with a jerk. 'Now?'

'A mother has been asking about her son.'

'Now?'

'Normally they don't ring until the raid is over.'

'Well?'

'His name's Fischer. Saturn gun. Killed by a bursting gun barrel.'

The lieutenant flinched. 'Have you told her that?'

'No.'

'So?'

'I said he was wounded.'

'Are you mad?' shouted the lieutenant.

'I wanted to do it slowly!' The operator stammered: 'I – thought . . .'

'What?'

'She should be told slowly.'

'So how did you do that?'

'Hung up,' said the operator. 'I hung up.'

The lieutenant threw his cigarette on the concrete floor. It went out in a puddle with a hiss. 'You're for it now.'

'Lieutenant?'

The phone rang. Without turning around, the operator picked up the receiver. 'Bertha Three, command post!'

There was a moment's silence, then the operator held out the receiver across the table. 'I've got the commanding officer on the line. He wants to speak to you.'

The lieutenant shook his head.

'But the commanding officer wants you!' The operator's voice rang out through the bunker. The lieutenant clenched his teeth, then he reached for the receiver. 'Bertha Three. Duty officer Lieutenant Wieninger.'

'Are the men on their way to the Americans?' came a voice from the earpiece.

'Major!' The lieutenant was silent for a moment. 'No, but straight away, Major.'

'It's important that nothing happens to the Americans. Do you understand that? I'm the commander in charge here.'

'Are you thinking, Major, about reprisals by the civilian population?' asked the lieutenant.

'I wouldn't like to express an opinion on that.'

'Could I draw your attention to the fact that the squad is in grave danger during the raid. The whole . . .'

'I didn't ask you about that.'

'Major, these are my men we're talking about!'

'Keep quiet. I'm giving you an order. Do you understand?'

'Yes, sir!'

'I didn't say you had to go yourself.'

'Over and out, Major,' said the lieutenant, and put down the receiver. He looked at the operator. 'Did you hear that?'

'No, I didn't hear a thing.'

'Then you're a lucky man.' The lieutenant turned around and walked to the door. 'Now I'm going to muster the men for the squad. Just so that you know.'

'Sir!'

The wireless operator wiped his face with his handkerchief. He rubbed at a patch of soot on his forehead. In doing so he distributed all the dirt evenly over his nose. When the other man had closed the door behind him, he walked over to it and bolted it shut.

Frau Cheovksi whispered: 'We've got to take something with us.'

'What?' he asked, and put his arm around her shoulder. They were both squatting by the wall. His suit was covered in dust.

'The memory,' she said. 'It was lovely, and now we're paying for it.'

'Don't talk like that.' He pressed her to him. Her breath was warm on his face. When he glanced at her, she was looking through him. Something red flitted across her cheeks. Not blood. The glow came from outside. Through the window frame it was reflected in the facade opposite.

He said: 'The house is on fire.'

She smiled. 'It doesn't matter.' Her hand stroked his arm. He felt her ring through the fabric. The red glow brightened. A feeling of unease crept over him. All at once he knew what fear was.

'Think about Walter and Rudolf!' She looked towards the table. 'I can see them sitting there.'

He did not reply and saw only the empty window. The glow

of fire flickered across it. It lit up, faded away and then flared up again. Wood crackled in the distance. Perhaps in a room.

'Let's go downstairs,' he suggested suddenly. He looked at her, but she wasn't listening.

'Please!'

'He was always a good child, and Rudolf was so proud,' she said.

It was a passage like a tunnel, only narrower. They couldn't walk side by side. Moisture seeped from the walls, a sour smell hung in the air, there were puddles on the floor. At the end of the passageway, a door.

'In there,' the soldier ordered. The metal tag dangled on his chest. The glow of his lamp flitted across the floor.

'Please!' The man turned around. 'I might have some cigarettes on me. Would you take cigarettes?'

The soldier gave a laugh and said nothing. He looked at the roof of the cellar. It creaked. A roll of thunder ran through the passageway. Spiders' webs stirred. After a few seconds it was quiet again.

'Open the door!'

The man pushed on the handle. The hinges squeaked. A candle-glow fell through the crack. The smell of wine reached him. They were sitting on the barrels. A whole troop of drunken soldiers.

'We've made an arrest!' came a voice behind the man. 'He tried to get away!'

A rifle butt cracked on the cobbles. The soldier was holding the weapon next to his right foot. The man opposite him dangled his legs.

'Lieutenant,' began the man. 'I . . .'

'I'm only an ensign!'

The others grinned. Their boots drummed against the barrels. One of them was smoking. A face like a child, freckles on his nose. The man said: 'Forgive me, but I've got to be on my way immediately!'

'Nothing to forgive!' The ensign slipped from his barrel. He was no older than the others. He reached thoughtfully for his submachine gun, where it was leaning against the wall, and weighed it in his hand.

'Are you in a hurry?'

'Yes, very much so.'

'So are we!'

Giggles accompanied his answer. Someone coughed deliberately. They were starting to enjoy themselves.

The man said: 'My child.'

Then they all laughed.

He looked at them, one after the other. They reminded him of his class in school.

'Here's my identification card.' He reached into his pocket. It was empty. Startled, he stopped.

'Go on, show us!'

'I've lost it,' the man answered, confused. They laughed loudly. The soldier with the cigarette burned his fingers on it. He pulled at his ear.

'I'm going!' All of a sudden the man turned around and headed for the door. His hand was reaching out when a corporal quickly struck his arm with the butt of his gun. It burned like fire.

'I remember you from school,' laughed the ensign.

The man turned around. Tears ran down his cheeks. He looked at the door.

A voice said: 'The state of him!'

The ensign walked around him and stood in front of him. He raised his arm, but he didn't strike. The man flinched, and they started laughing again.

'He limps, too,' said the corporal.

'I . . .'

The ensign asked unpleasantly: 'Going looting, were you?' One of the soldiers on the barrels suggested: 'We could hand-cuff him.'

The man said: 'I beg you in the name of God . . .'

'Stand by the wall!'

'In God's name!' The man wiped the tears away. 'Please!'

'We don't believe in God!'

Now they were roaring with laughter.

'By the wall!' the ensign ordered.

The man obeyed. He limped to the wall.

'Arse towards us!' The ensign took out his handkerchief and blew his nose into it. 'Or do I have to say backside?' he asked. The man stared at the stones. They gleamed with moisture. He listened for sounds outside, but heard nothing.

'My child,' he whispered.

'Shut it!' yelled the ensign.

They struck their boots against the barrels. This was tremendous fun.

The two thousand volts hadn't killed him. There was no power in the lines. Sergeant Strenehen hit the pylon like a sack.

He slid down the iron rungs. It planed the skin from his left hand. Barbed wire tore his trousers off, diagonally across the seat. Then he touched the ground.

Almost delicately. He broke two ribs without noticing. Twenty feet above him the parachute flapped between the copper wires, in a storm unleashed by the flames. The straps were torn. There was nothing but fire all around him. Strenehen thought: I'm going to burn to death.

He had fallen into an electricity transformer, but he didn't know that. Seething oil boiled in tanks. He thought it was water. There was a stench of mustard. Rubber crackled like bacon. Jonathan Strenehen sat on warm metal with his bare backside. It was the north side of a tin roof, blown there by the wind. The holster of his pistol bumped against it. He took out the weapon and threw it away. If he was unarmed there was nothing they could do to him. The Germans. He craved other people.

The pistol discharged with a crack in the midst of the flames. A bullet whizzed over his head.

And then the next one went off, as though they were trying to kill him. He waited for the last, but it didn't come. Maybe he'd miscounted.

When he made out a gap in the flames, he got to his feet and stumbled towards it. With his left hand he held his shirt closed in front of his belly, for modesty's sake.

People, he thought. Someone somewhere must still be alive. He was engulfed in smoke.

The road led diagonally across the graveyard. The bombs ploughed it up like a field. A stick of bombs brought down some trees. They burst out of their bark.

In the trench they felt only the tremor.

Chikin asked: 'What's that?'

White fluid ran from Nikolai's sleeve and dripped to the ground.

'Pus!'

Chikin choked on his strap. Smoke swelled through the bare shrubs and came towards them. A cloud. He asked: 'Catch it from Rastyeva?'

'Yes!'

The drumming on the street stopped. A tree was burning like a torch. The wood crackled. 'We should have reported Rastyeva,' he said. 'We'll all get infected.'

'Too late for me!'

Bluebottles swarmed over the grass. They had been startled and were in search of fresh food. Fat and glittering, they buzzed over Chikin's leg. He pulled the strap through his teeth. 'What are you going to do?'

'Nothing!' Nikolai Petrovich raised his shoulders. 'After medical examination they'll send me to a camp.'

Smoke rolled over the trench like a black cloth. The air grew dry. Rastyeva started to cough up blood and mucus. He vomited with a groan.

'There is one possibility,' said Chikin. The fluid from the strap ran down his chin.

'What?'

'Cauterise!'

One of the flies crept over Chikin's mouth. It sucked up saliva. He flicked it away.

'And what about Rastyeva?'

'We'll have to report him.'

With a loud roar a delayed-action bomb blew up the street. Earth clattered on top of them. It came like hail through the smoke. When it was over, peace settled everywhere. The smoke rolled away.

'We've never reported anyone.'

'No,' Chikin confirmed.

The burning tree toppled over. It fell like a human being. Upright. Dry foliage scattered. Every leaf was singed.

'Do you think,' Nikolai asked, 'they'll carry out an investigation?'

'Who can say? I've seen Germans shaving before an air-raid.'

Singing came from the distance. It was like the mooing of a herd of cattle, the clear voices of the young ones in between.

'Do you hear it?' asked Chikin.

'Yes.'

The wind brought screams. They rang out through the drone of the bombers.

'People!'

'Very close by,' added Nikolai. He took the board and threw it at Rastyeva's feet. They listened. Chikin forgot to chew. The strap slipped from between his teeth. Between the organ blast of the guns the voices rang out.

Nikolai whispered: 'We'll have to do something.'

'To hell with them!'

Chikin took the strap and wrapped it around his belly. He tied a knot.

Rastyeva turned his head to one side. 'We might find something to eat.' His chin sank back on his chest.

'Are you coming?' Nikolai looked at Chikin. He was playing with his strap. The drone of the aeroplane engines grew louder. Bombs began to whistle.

'But not for the food.'

'Come on!'

Nikolai stood up. He climbed over the edge of the ditch, using the board on Rastyeva's feet as a step. The bombs tore

the ground two hundred yards away. Explosions boomed.
Dirt sprayed. He ran away. Chikin grabbed Rastyeva by the
sleeve. He pulled him up. They helped each other over the
parapet.

'Now we'll get some bread,' giggled Rastyeva.

In the meadow they embraced like brothers. Arms linked,
they were about to go on. Something whistled – they were
both torn apart on the spot. The flesh came away from their
bones. Rastyeva's arm hurled through the air. The chewed
strap burst. A second later a crater gaped where they had
been standing. Their blood didn't even seep into the earth,
because it vaporised.

Nikolai Petrovich turned around. He saw it. Then he
walked on.

'Don't you talk to me about good sense,' said the widow. 'My
husband did his duty, with loyalty and courage. He is a dead
hero. A lot of good that'll do him.'

'You talk too much,' replied the man.

They were talking in the dark. The candle had gone out.
The air smelt like the air in a grave. The others listened.

'So, then?' asked the man. 'Are we going to dig ourselves
out now?'

'Of course,' rang a voice from the darkness. 'We've been
waiting for four hours.'

The widow fired back: 'How do you know that?'

'I've got an alarm clock.'

'She's got an alarm clock,' said the widow. 'We ask what
time it is a hundred times, and she's got an alarm clock.'

'Show us!' the man ordered.

'You can't see it.' The voice began to wheeze. It was giggling.

'Hear it, then,' replied the widow. 'Let's hear it.'

'Tick, tock,' said the voice. 'Tick, tock!'

The man picked up a stone and threw it into the darkness. It struck a body. The old woman in the corner suddenly cried out: 'My Fredi's come back to life! He moved!'

'Madness,' said the widow. 'They're all crazy down here.'

'Please,' said a voice from the bench. 'Control yourself. The only crazy person here is you.'

'What do you mean?' the widow asked menacingly.

'Let's not have an argument,' said the man. 'We've had enough arguments.'

There was silence for a while. For an hour or a minute. A constant rhythmic panting came through the darkness. After a while someone said: 'I'm not having this.'

'What?'

'This breathing. She's using up our air with the gas-mask.'

'Take the mask off her!' ordered the man.

There was a gurgled reply, but the mechanical panting continued.

'If she doesn't take the mask off . . .' the widow asserted, 'I'll pull it off her!'

'You do that!' the old woman from the corner announced with satisfaction.

She said: 'Fredi hasn't got a mask either.'

'Fredi!' mimicked the woman. 'Fredi!'

'You horrible woman,' whispered the voice that had previously requested self-control.

'My love!' The widow sniffed audibly. 'I don't even know where my husband is buried. I can say what I like.'

'Don't forget there's a war on,' replied the man.

The people on the bench guffawed derisively. The man

said nothing. The breathing through the gas-mask filter remained the only sound.

Suddenly someone said: 'You've killed the girl.'

'Nonsense!' the man gasped.

'No, you have!'

'I only knocked her out.'

'She's been out for hours. You don't even believe that yourself.'

The man whispered: 'It's what you wanted. I got her to shut up.'

'No one wanted it,' answered the widow.

'Of course they did!' There was a crash as the man struck his hand furiously on the stones.

A gloating voice came from the bench: 'If she's dead, it was murder.'

'You'll be executed,' added the widow. She announced proudly: 'I'm a witness!'

'God damn it!' shouted the man. 'You incited me to do it!'

Right then a clear voice asked: 'Where am I?'

It was the girl. They all held their breath. All but the woman with the gas-mask. They heard her moving. The girl sat up.

'I knew it straight away,' the widow cried with satisfaction. 'She's alive!'

'Fredi's alive!' The old woman from the corner suddenly scrambled to her feet and shook the beam. The wood creaked.

'Stop!' It was a single shout, but it came too late. The wall next to the corpse came down. Stones fell. The vaulting collapsed.

'Save yourselves!' roared the man. Springing up, he crashed into a body and then against the door. When the stones settled he was lying on a human being. It was the girl. They heard nothing more from the others. They were alone in a cave.

The priest was no different from the others now. He lay on the ground. His legs were crushed under a girder. He couldn't feel a thing. His pain went unfelt. In five minutes at most he would burn to death. He thought: That's the reward for being keen.

His voice was swallowed by the smoke as though by fog. He had had no practice at shouting. Praying seemed pointless now. He thought: No one will hear me.

His sins came to mind. They made him laugh. He laughed loudly and desperately. He lay on the cobbles like an old woman. His habit had rucked up, and he wore trousers underneath.

If I'm a saint, I'll get a shirt, he thought. Suddenly he was as simple as a child. He remembered the cross. He wanted to burn to death with the cross in his hand. A saint dies according to the rules.

He thought: If there is a God, he'll have to make his presence felt now. Maybe out of the flames. A fatherly voice filled with love.

The priest listened to the fire. Crackling wood. That was all.

He began to shout again. This time he was shouting out of fear, only to calm himself down. He used to hope he wouldn't have to die alone.

The veins in the priest's forehead swelled, he was shouting so much. He had four times sixty seconds left. He set a record in shouting. Before he burned to death.

VI

I was ordained as a priest in Freising on 28 June 1932. The stations of my pastoral activity so far have been: Augsburg, Kaplan in Barmen and Expositus in Cologne. A year ago I was transferred to this city. In my sermons I have always referred to the dangers of unbelief. I have demanded of the educated above all that they should work for faith by word and example. Four days ago I wrote to the Cardinal: By the time you receive this letter, my body may no longer exist. But I am happy in Jesus!

Thus the heart of my Master, the loving Christ who is near me, makes me so happy that he comforts me in all things. I pray and believe. He will not let me fall.

The American plane dived steeply. Muzzle flash lit up its wings. In one second eight fixed machine guns fired 580 rounds at the platform of the flak tower. A shadow flitted across the concrete. Ricochets twittered like birds through the air. Suction whirled up dust. The gun commander flinched. He felt a blow to his leg. A moment later the fighter was already flashing over the roofs and disappearing.

He closed the door. The metal boomed. An iron staircase led downstairs. His feet hammered on the steps. It grew cold. Fresh air rushed towards him. A light was on in the room. There was still peace here.

The engineer panted: 'Hey, where have you come from?'

In English: '*Thanks*!'

The engineer shouted: 'Stein, help! An American!'

He leapt to the wall in alarm. The stranger looked at the ceiling. It was a control room. Copper rails ran along the walls. A door flew open. A man with an iron bar rushed in. He was dressed like an engineer.

'*I haven't got a gun*!'

'What did he say?'

'I don't understand English.' The engineer shut his gaping mouth.

'Hands up!'

The American raised his right arm, clumsily wiggled his left hand and shrugged his shoulders. He was naked from his shoes to his belt.

'You are a prisoner,' said the mechanic, in German. 'Resistance is pointless.' He put the iron bar on the ground. It clanked.

'*Thanks*!'

An impact shook the ceiling. The engineer opened his mouth once more, and closed it again. He had said nothing. All three raised their heads.

'Cigarette?' the mechanic asked suddenly.

'*Do you understand me*?'

The mechanic took a case from his pocket.

'*Thanks*!'

'Hand-rolled.'

'*Prima*!' said the American, in the mechanic's language.

'He speaks German, boss!'

The engineer straightened his tie and threw his head back. 'You speak German?'

'War nix good,' said the American.

The engineer pointed quickly at the ceiling. He shouted furiously: 'Alles kaputt!'

'*Very much!*' the American agreed. His face was covered with a layer of soot. His eyes gleamed. He brought down his right arm, covered his nakedness and spat on the floor.

'No spitting in here,' said the engineer.

The mechanic took out his lighter and clicked it at the American's cigarette.

'*Thank you!*'

'My name's Stein.' The mechanic began to smile, and the American smiled too. They sat down on a copper rail. The American folded his arms over his lap. There was blood on his left knee.

'Careful,' whispered the engineer. 'He may be armed.'

'No, his holster's empty.' The mechanic whispered too. 'I looked inside it.' Suddenly he said in a normal voice: 'What he most urgently needs is a pair of trousers.'

'We can't let him have them.'

'Why not?'

'You know why not!'

The mechanic lit himself a cigarette, blew the smoke to the ceiling and said nothing. There were noises over by the metal door. But nothing happened. The mechanic studied the American from the side.

The American pointed to his arm, and said in English: '*It's broken!*'

'Stein,' said the engineer. 'Kill him!'

'*You can't see it, though.*'

'Me?'

The engineer said: 'I can't do it. I used to keep rabbits, but I always gave them away to be slaughtered.'

The mechanic stared at the floor. The clouds of smoke floated to the ceiling. The American threw his cigarette on to the concrete and stamped it out. He was being wasteful, even though he had no socks on.

'I've got an idea,' said the engineer.

'What?'

'I'm going to electrify the rails.'

'And what about me?'

'You stay here and make sure he doesn't stand up.'

'But he's a nice enough fellow,' replied the mechanic. 'Why do you want to kill him?'

The engineer looked at the ceiling. 'Because he helped to kill my wife; with his bombs.'

The mechanic looked at the American. 'The Lord sayeth: Vengeance is mine.'

'Fine,' agreed the engineer. 'Vengeance is mine. I am the Lord!'

The gun commander on the platform of the bunker rolled sideways. He felt his leg, then raised his right hand. His hand was smeared with blood. Blood clung between his fingers, blood ran from his wrist and down the elbow into the sleeve. His arm fell back. His palm struck the concrete. Making a great effort, he turned his head to one side. The tendons in his neck tensed. The loader lay motionless beside him. His eyes were closed. He looked as though he were asleep. Blood was still running from under the bandage around his face. The trickle came from behind his ear, dripped on to the concrete and mixed with the dust.

The gun commander tried to pull in a leg, but it wouldn't obey. With his left hand he felt for his chin and slowly lifted his head higher. The gunners were less than ten feet away. He saw their pale faces under their helmets, their eyes wide open. They stared at him.

He tried to speak, but no sound came from his lips. His mouth moved silently. His lips formed the words twice, when suddenly the three gunners reached for the straps around their bodies. They hauled themselves upright. With feverish fingers they undid the knots. Almost as one they leapt forwards. They jumped to the ladder at the edge of the platform. Two paces from the abyss the strongest of them pulled the other two back. The strongest one swung on to the iron rungs. He climbed down fast. His head disappeared.

The other two watched him listlessly. Then they returned to their straps, tied themselves in and lay back down on the concrete.

The gun commander's head had dropped forward. Beside his leg a sunbeam fell onto a pool of blood. Thin haze rose up. A fly, dazed by smoke and gunpowder, wobbled through the air. It tumbled down on to the puddle, fell into the thick mass, tipped sideways and lay there with its legs in the air. The thin stalks moved helplessly in the void.

There was no one there to give the two gunners an order, so they closed their eyes.

There was a glow on the wall. It entered the room through the empty window frames. Sunset, thought Herr Cheovski. But it was fire. Flames lit the facade. He felt the heat on his back. His wife crouched on the floor. He knelt in front of her.

'Get up, Dessy!'

'Leave me alone,' she whispered.

'Come on – we can't do this.'

Her eyes reminded him of glass balls.

'What?' she asked.

'Stay here.'

Frau Cheovski said in a changed voice: 'If you don't want to stay, then go!'

'Without you, never!'

'No?'

'Never, Dessy,' said Herr Cheovksi, then got to his feet and looked at the door. He saw the door, the door, the door . . .

The NCO pulled the strap with the headphones off his shoulder, handed it to a gunner and jumped on to the parapet. 'What's going on?' he asked.

'Three men,' said the lieutenant, 'for a mission.' He looked into the sky. His shirt clung to his back. It was wet. He could see nothing overhead. The layer of haze lay over the gun emplacement. He stared into it.

'What for?' asked the NCO.

'What do you think?'

A flash lit up the trench. The gun barrel rose. It boomed. The lieutenant quickly held his right hand in front of his face.

'What for?' shouted the NCO.

'Don't shout like that!'

A scar ran over the NCO's forehead. He touched it with his fingers. 'I thought you were still deaf.'

'Not any more.'

'What do you need the men for?'

'I've had an order.'

'I thought you weren't going to obey that order?'

The lieutenant lowered his head and looked the NCO in the eyes. 'How do you know that?'

'We heard it.'

'On the radio?'

'Yes, your operator didn't switch it off. All the gun commanders heard it.'

The lieutenant looked into the emplacement. The gun with the exploded barrel looked like a tree-stump. Two gunners were carrying parts of a man on their shovels. They ran with the stuff and carried it between them, as though walking a tightrope. By the parapet they dumped it on to a tarpaulin. Flesh and hair. A piece of gut fell beside it. They busily scraped it all together. The NCO pointed towards the city. 'Do you think I'm going to give up my men for something like that?'

The lieutenant looked at the ground. 'Orders are orders, what can you do?'

'Where's the commanding officer?'

'In his bunker.'

'Ten feet of concrete,' said the NCO. 'He's had his war, now he's thinking about the peace.'

'It's all about human lives, after all.'

'Exactly.' In a single movement the NCO jumped, legs apart, into the trench. He fell to his knees and shouted: 'To hell with honour!' His words echoed through the emplacement for a second before the salvo, then the guns replied.

There was nothing for it, the lieutenant would have to go to the next emplacement. He turned away irritably. He's right, of course, he thought. What's to be done?

Sparks lashed down on them like glowing hail. Heads drawn in, hands shielding their faces, they ran for their lives down a street that had shrunk to a footpath, while a hurricane raged about them. The wet blankets flapped on their shoulders.

There was no sky now. Four-storey frontages burned to right and left. They ran through curtains of ash, leapt over flames and waded through shards of glass that crunched beneath their feet like splintered ice.

The man on the mountain of rubble saw them coming and stumbled towards them.

He waved his arms in the air. With his cuirassier's helmet on his head he looked like someone dressed for carnival. The fire was reflected in the brass.

'Save her!' he roared.

'Who?'

'Emma!'

'Where?'

'Here!'

Suddenly the man whined like a dog. 'She's under there!'

He pointed to the rubble. Smouldering beams stuck out of tiles. A strong wind swept over them. The leader of the unit pushed the man out of his way.

'Go on!'

Swaddled figures wrapped in blankets dashed past, along the rubble. The smoke swallowed them up.

Legs splayed, the man stood on the path. Flailing his arms like windmills, he hoped to stop the next people who came. But no one came. Tears drew runnels through the ash-dust on his face. The cuirassier's helmet wobbled on his head. The man sobbed. His body turned around on its own axis and he crept up the pile of rubble. He picked up the smoking debris with his hands. He began to scrabble. Faster and faster. Embers scattered in the air. The storm took hold of the fire, and flames licked all around the mountain of rubble. Like a clown, with his helmet as a mask, the man dug. He was looking for the entrance to a cellar.

★

'Are you still alive?'

He grabbed the girl by the face, touched her nose. The darkness was impenetrable.

'Are you still alive?' he repeated.

'Yes.'

The girl whispered. The strange hand ran over her lips. A finger went into her mouth. The man lay on top of her. His breath blew through her hair. She could feel his body.

The man panted: 'I want to know if you're still alive!' He said to himself: 'She's still warm. If you're warm you're still alive.' He pressed himself against her.

'Please stop . . .' The girl turned her head. Her throat was sore. Her chin was pressed against his chest. His shirt was open. She felt the hairs on her lips. The man gave a groan.

'Stop, please,' she said. 'I'm alive!'

'You're alive?' The man seemed astonished. Convulsively he grabbed her forehead. He asked doubtfully: 'You're alive?'

'Yes!'

Suddenly he whispered: 'Who are you?'

'You're crushing me!' His other arm lay between her body and his. His elbow dug into her stomach.

'Who are you?'

'But you know me!'

She reached into the darkness and touched his shoulder. She felt bones beneath the fabric. 'Injured?'

'No!' he answered harshly.

A drop of saliva from his mouth fell on her forehead. He was choking. It reached his chest.

'Get up!' she begged.

'I can't!' He reared up, slumped back. His weight fell on her body. In a normal voice he said: 'We're trapped.'

'Help!' she shouted all of a sudden. 'Help!'

Then she started to cry.

'Don't do that,' he said. 'They can't hear us.'

'Be quiet! Can you hear something?'

'What?' He held his breath. The girl gasped. They both listened.

'Nothing,' he said.

'Are we going to die?'

'Of course not!' He started to giggle silently. She could feel him trembling. It shook his body. He smelt of tobacco.

'And the air?' she asked tearfully.

'There's air. Enough air. I can feel it.' He blew in her face.

The girl breathed more deeply.

'Slowly,' he ordered. His voice sounded like a doctor's.

'Can you move?'

'I'm going to try!' He raised his head, slowly pulled out his arm. Below her breasts his hand ran over her body. Her dress was torn. She could feel his fingers. It was easier when his arm was no longer between them. She reached up, into the void. 'There's room there.'

'Not enough to stand up.'

Lying on top of her, he started to wriggle. She waited. His head came down. When his body was lying still again she breathed out.

'You know, as a boy,' he began, 'I once crawled down a pipe. It was just like this.'

'And?' asked the girl.

'I didn't get stuck, of course.' He fell silent, as though considering something, then started to clear his throat. His body grew heavier. He lay on her breasts like an animal. Fear threatened to suffocate her. She suddenly sensed that he desired her.

She asked: 'Are your parents still alive?' She was almost shouting.

'No!'

'Your wife?' she asked hastily.

'I'm a widower.'

'Children?'

'One daughter. What has that got to do with you?'

'I'm the same age as your daughter,' she answered quickly.

'No!' Unmoved, he said: 'My daughter's older.'

His foot tensed. He pressed it against her thigh.

'I'll scream!'

'Do that!' He retreated a little, but from his wheezing she could tell that he was getting ready. I've got to wait, she felt. Wait! She waited for what was coming. In the silence she heard dull rumbling, then she also felt movement. The earth was being bombed.

She wondered: How many days have I been lying here?

She didn't know.

The door opened. The engineer came in and said: 'It won't work!'

The American sat on the rail. He didn't understand a word.

'Won't it?' asked the mechanic.

'There's no current. You're going to have to hit him over the head.'

'No current?' The mechanic pointed at the ceiling. 'If the lights are on, there's current.'

'That's the battery.'

The mechanic looked at the rails and thought. The American quickly pressed his legs together. The rail was narrow. He wanted to stand up, but he was too ashamed. He could bear it sitting down. He had to speak to distract the others. He said, in English: '*I don't feel well.*'

'What did he say?'

'How should I know?'

The engineer leaned against the door. He drummed his fingers against the door panel. There was a sign above his head. The American couldn't read it. He leaned forwards. The mechanic looked at the American's backside. The American was happier with the German looking at his backside than at his genitals.

'Hit him on the head now, with the iron bar,' said the engineer. 'Then it'll be over quickly.'

A stone pinged. It bounced down the stairs through the middle of the room. It came to a stop in the corner. It was a pebble. The iron bar leaned against the wall.

'Do we have to?' asked the mechanic. 'Leave that kind of thing to other people.'

'An eye for an eye. A tooth for a tooth.'

The mechanic asked: 'How's it going, my friend?'

The American suddenly held a hand below his navel.

'*I don't like this!*' he said and splayed his fingers.

'Not another word. I'll give you the order. Officially!'

In three steps the engineer reached the wall, picked up the iron bar and held it out. 'Prove you're a man!'

The mechanic's chin jutted forwards. He wiped it with his hand, then took the bar. He weighed it in his hands. It was square at the end. He tested an edge with his thumb.

'Come on!' The engineer went to the door and pushed

down the handle. 'When you've finished' – he stepped over the threshold – 'knock.'

The door slammed shut. Plaster trickled from the panel and scattered on the floor.

The mechanic looked at the sign on the door. He read: *Only authorised personnel are permitted to enter this control room.*

'That's impossible!' The lance corporal waved his hand. 'I need all of them.'

The lieutenant asked furiously: 'Are you the officer on duty here, or am I?' Smoke swirled around his feet.

'You are, of course.'

'Then you obey me.'

The lance corporal touched his hand to his helmet. The lieutenant suspected he was laughing at him. Loaders ran around them. They were carrying bags of powder for the cartridges.

The lieutenant said: 'Two men, right now.'

'Sorry!' The lance corporal shrugged his shoulders. 'Then we'd have to stop firing!' Now he looked like a waiter. The lieutenant asked: 'What do you do for a living?'

'I'm a variety artiste.'

'I don't believe it.' The veins in the lieutenant's temples stood out. He turned red in the face.

'Fire!' shouted the lance corporal.

The gun flashed. Smoke and noise engulfed them. When it subsided the lance corporal knelt on the base plate and fiddled with a charge.

The lieutenant kicked the cartridge. It fell over.

'Stand up!'

'Charge two!' roared the lance corporal to the loaders. Then he said: 'Who gave the order?'

'What?'

The lance corporal stood up. 'I wasn't talking to you.'

He turned away. The lieutenant looked at his back. He was tempted to thump him, but he went on his way. I'll have that man, he thought.

The ensign took the flask and put it to his lips. He tilted back his head and drank greedily. It glugged through his throat, then he choked. The yellow wine bubbled out under his nose. His whole chin was sticky. The drops glittered in the beam of light.

'Ha, ha!' He laughed and turned around. 'A drop for the delinquent as well?'

The man by the wall stood still and stared at the stones. Moss grew in abundance on the stone blocks. A spider ran away at incredible speed. He had breathed on it. On its back was a cross. The man thought: a cross spider. It was a mechanical thought.

'Schnapps is good for cholera,' a voice drawled. The soldier struck an empty barrel with the butt of his rifle. It boomed. The man was immediately alert. Then he realised his mistake and looked back at the stones. Pale green moss. It reminded him of Easter. He had made nests out of paper grass. One of them was left by the window. The sun came, the chocolate melted, his child cried. Tears over nothing. He had smiled at that. There was no sun here.

'Do you want a drop, or do you not want a drop?' The ensign leaned forward drunkenly. Beads glittered on his forehead. He was sweating in spite of the cold of the room.

The man said: 'Please, let me go!'

'Hell!' One of the ensign's feet stamped on the cobbles. The heel of his boot came away from the sole. Iron clanked against the wall. The ensign stared at him.

A voice announced: 'He's determined to kill himself.'

'My God!' A soldier laughed. 'You're safe here. What do you think is happening out there?'

'You have to understand. My child . . .'

'Shut up!' roared the ensign.

'Schnapps is good for cholera!' A voice like a girl's. It was just breaking, and sounded adolescent. Hopelessly childish. The bayonet clanked.

The ensign said: 'Shut up now. We're on duty, people!' Then he threw up. Wine and half-digested food splashed on to the floor. His face grew pasty. A sour smell spread.

'I couldn't agree more!' cried a member of the troop. Then he sat on his barrel and babbled incomprehensibly. They were all terribly cheerful. The safety catch of a pistol kept clicking. Someone was playing with it. Open. Shut. Open. It clicked through the shouting.

'I feel better for that!' The ensign hawked up the mucus in his throat. It gurgled and he spat it out. He wiped his mouth on his sleeve. When he was finished he ordered: 'Clean it up!'

'Who?' asked the soldier with the breaking voice.

'The delinquent, of course!'

The man at the wall took a deep breath. 'If you let me go afterwards,' he announced, 'I'll happily clean it up.'

'Haggler!' The ensign laughed. 'So, men, are we open to negotiations?'

'Yes,' they all drawled, even the ones who didn't know what was going on.

The man tried to turn around. He turned on his shortened leg.

'Halt!' ordered the ensign. 'Not so fast.'

His hand brought the flask to his mouth. 'First I have to rinse!' He stood in the middle of his vomit, swaying back and forth. The vomit spread in all directions.

The man looked at the wall again. He calculated: four minutes to the station. I need one minute to perform my task. In five minutes I'll be there. In three hundred seconds I'll know if my child is alive. My child must be alive. 'Now!' ordered the ensign's voice. The man turned around. They were all standing there. The whole troop standing around the vomit. They looked at it.

'Now, my friend,' said the ensign, 'show us what you can do.'

The man looked at the puddle. It was slimy. A piece of half-digested sausage sat in the middle. He took two steps forwards. He thought for a second, then unbuttoned his jacket. He slipped an arm out of one sleeve, pulled the jacket over his shoulder, fell on his knees and wiped away with his jacket. They watched his work like experts. No one said a word until he had finished. He stood up again, not even feeling nauseous.

The ensign started twinkling. 'And my boots.'

The man took out his handkerchief, then bent down and wiped the boots clean as well. When he stood up this time, he walked straight to the door.

'Halt!' called the ensign. 'Where do you think you're going?'

'I've got to get to the station!'

'The trains aren't running.' The ensign wiped his mouth

with his arm. He yawned. 'And anyway I have to take everything into consideration. If you loot, you get shot. If there was no justice, where would we be?'

A drunken voice agreed: 'Quite right.'

The man saw stars. He clutched his heart.

VII

I, Viktor Lutz, born on 24 November 1921, ensign with a special commando, shot my first man on the road between Chudovo and Novo-Selje, half a mile out of Chudovo. It's four miles from Chudovo to Novo-Selje. There were forty prisoners. They couldn't go any further, and I was alone. As we had no language that we could communicate in, they pointed mutely at their chests. Each gesture became a request for death. I only brought one of them to Novo-Selje. He confirmed that I had killed the others. After that I had to shoot him behind a cabin. He had one arm in a sling. That was the start of my career. Fatherland, heroism, tradition, honour are all so many slogans. They sent me on to the road from Novo-Selje with slogans.

The mechanic put his index finger to his mouth.

Strenehen shrugged. He didn't know what was going on.

The other German had closed the door with the sign on it behind him. The light-bulb was dimming. No one said anything. The dull light cast no shadows. A dull murmur came from up above.

'Stand up!' whispered the mechanic. He lifted the iron bar from the floor. Carefully, as though he didn't want to make a sound. Strenehen looked at him uncomprehendingly.

'Get up!'

'*What?*'

The mechanic beckoned to him, without a word.

Strenehen understood. He got to his feet.

The mechanic glanced at the sign on the door and crept towards the stairs. He walked like a cat.

'*What's going on?*' Strenehen pulled at his shirt. He leaned forward, to make his shirt longer.

'Psst!'

The mechanic pointed to his lips again. He climbed three

steps. He stopped there and turned around. He raised the iron bar. It was an invitation. He beckoned.

'*Okay*!' Strenehen stepped forwards, but suddenly he stopped. He stood in the middle of the room. His face was covered with scratches.

'Come on,' whispered the mechanic.

He looked back sharply, rolling his eyes. There was a distant rumble. Strenehen stepped hesitantly closer. He was shivering. There was gooseflesh on his thighs.

'Hurry up!'

The mechanic climbed up another step. Strenehen waited below him. The mechanic leaned the iron bar against his shoulder. He held it there like a weapon.

Strenehen raised his arm. '*No good*!'

The mechanic twitched back.

'*Nothing*!' replied Strenehen and shook his head. He wanted nothing from him.

'Come on!' The mechanic climbed another step.

Strenehen asked loudly: '*What's going on?*'

'Shut up!' whispered the mechanic. He beckoned again with his hand, then climbed on.

He stood sideways, concentrating on both Strenehen and the stairs. He walked carefully.

Strenehen followed him. He climbed cautiously. Perhaps the stairs were unsafe. For no particular reason he counted the steps. None of it made any sense. The man above him, clutching his iron bar, was acting mysteriously. The pain in Strenehen's arm returned. While he had been sitting down he hadn't felt a thing. The mechanic kept climbing. When he reached the door, he turned around again. Strenehen could clearly hear explosions. A veil of white smoke was forcing its way in between the threshold and the door. The air was hot.

'Come. Now!'

Strenehen stepped up. He stood beside the mechanic on the same step. The room lay beneath them, in semi-darkness. The mechanic gripped the handle. Suddenly he pushed the door open.

Strenehen saw smoke. Outside, twenty feet in front of him, something was boiling. Flames darted up. He felt a shove in the back. He stumbled forwards, outside. Before he turned around, the door was locked behind him. It was a flat surface of grey iron at the top of a concrete plinth leading diagonally out of the ground. The door sealed the plinth.

'*Damn*!' shouted Strenehen. He hurled himself against the door, drumming with his fists. '*Open the door! Open the door!*'

He didn't understand. There was a fire behind him. Guns pounded.

'*Fucking German*!' he shouted.

Exhausted, he turned around and looked at the sky. Fear paralysed him, contorted his face. A mile above him he saw the dots of a stick of bombs whirling towards him. He stood by the iron door as though crucified.

The anti-aircraft gunner stood on the last rung of the ladder. The iron trembled. He let go of the uprights. Jumped.

Next to the bunker a bomb had ploughed up the ground. He disappeared into the crater as though into a trench. His chin struck stones. He slid down. His back crashed against concrete. He splayed his legs. The water-pipe struck his genitals like a steel rod. The pain took his breath away. He gasped for air. For a minute he straddled the pipe, unable to move. He groaned.

His hair was filled with ashes. He had lost his helmet. A sunbeam gleamed in the crater like a headlamp. Smoke drifted by and extinguished the light. He was about to pull himself up the walls when the wailing began. A hundred sirens.

Firebombs. They whizzed through the air, hurtling towards the bunker, on to the street, on to the pavement. A moment later the air trembled. There was a drumming sound on the cobbles. Fire sprayed. Suddenly everything was on fire. A jet of flame shot into the sky.

The gunner crawled along the ground. He whispered: 'Mum.' Hot air enveloped him. That was all that happened. The gunner whimpered: 'Mum!'

What a beautiful city, thought Nikolai Petrovich. The fiery wind passed over his bald head. It was warm. He had thrown away his fur cap. He didn't run, he strolled, one step after the other, looking at everything. He thought: A man with nothing to lose doesn't run. A proverb occurred to him: If you lose time, don't bend down to get it or you'll lose some more. He'd heard that from Sinaida Blinova. Sinaida Blinova was dead. He didn't think about her.

The street led to the houses. They were in flames. Wood crackled. The street was as broad as Nevsky Prospekt. Nikolai imagined he was walking across Nevsky Prospekt. The Germans had built a big brick basin for fire-fighting water, but the basin was dry. A wall had collapsed and the water had flowed away. It had all evaporated in the heat. Not a beautiful city, thought Nikolai, and tried to laugh. All that emerged was a gurgle. He suddenly shouted: 'Rotten Germanskis!' He clenched his fist and threatened the flames, then spat. It wasn't worth it. There was no one there. They'd all slunk off.

The plinth of a monument stood in front of him. The ragged camouflage net lay around it, along with a fallen figure. It was made of metal. A man wearing a cycling cape. His arm was holding something. It had broken off. Nikolai stepped closer and opened his trousers. He sprayed the figure in the face with his jet of urine. The storm blew half of it against his leg. It ran warm against the inside of his thigh. When he had finished he sat on the metal man's feet. The metal man was wearing solid boots. Nikolai thought: have a little rest. Half a *verst* away bombs were exploding. He couldn't hear the screaming any more. He looked at the sky. Through the gaps in the smoke-clouds he saw aeroplanes. Their engines roared. A flak splinter whirred through the air. A hornet. Nikolai craned his neck after it. His thin neck. The tendons stood out. He got to his feet again. One of the houses was just collapsing. The building stood alone. It fell apart like a shed with four wooden walls. Each wall six storeys high. The facade fell in his direction. A huge cloud poured towards him. He closed his eyes. It sounded like the start of a landslide. The ground shook. Bits of wall rolled to his feet, then the storm drove the smoke on its way. Nothing but some sparks, which fell on his arm. He beat them away. He strolled slowly down the street, past rubble and smouldering heaps. Nikolai Petrovich was one of the living dead. He no longer dreamt of bread. The dead don't suffer from hunger.

'Why have you locked yourself in?' asked the lieutenant. He studied the walls. Nothing had changed.

The wireless operator replied: 'It wasn't on purpose.'

Instead of a bulb, a candle flickered. The mirror reflected the light, the lieutenant looked suspiciously at the table. Cigarette butts lay in a plate. That was all.

'Not on purpose?'

'No!' The operator fiddled with his set. A valve glowed. There was a whistling sound and the valve grew brighter. The guns boomed outside.

It was as though they were both standing on the deck of a ship. The floor kept shaking.

'Turn off the radio telephone!'

'Yes, sir!' The operator reached for a switch. Drops of water detached from the ceiling and fell into the radio. It hissed.

'Short-circuit?'

'No!' The operator pulled out his handkerchief. He wiped away in the gloom, then looked up. Beads of water hung from the concrete.

The lieutenant whispered: 'Will you switch that thing off?'

'It is switched off.'

'Sure?'

'Quite sure!' The operator gave a sideways glance. In the mirror he saw the lieutenant from behind. There was grass stuck to his shoulder.

'Have you any iron crosses left?'

The operator reached silently under the table. The drawer jammed. With a jerk he pulled it open, then put the paper bag on the table. It clanked.

The words on the bag read: *Eat fruit and stay healthy*.

'I wouldn't mind swapping you an Iron Cross First Class!' The operator coughed artfully and looked at the floor, glancing up at the lieutenant from below.

'How much for?'

'Eight packs of cigarettes.'

There was a silence.

'And a bottle of Moselle!' announced the operator triumphantly.

'Fine. But no certificate, I can't do that now.'

The lieutenant grabbed the bag, took out one Iron Cross and dropped it on the table.

'It doesn't matter!' the operator whispered. 'I'll pass it on through my brother-in-law, it's for a doctor. We talked about that before. It's . . .'

'Fine!' The lieutenant turned away impatiently.

He clamped the bag under his prosthesis and went to the door. He saw the wireless operator's face in the mirror. Their eyes met for a fraction of a second. As he opened the door the draught blew the candle out. In the dark the operator put the cross in his pocket. It was sticky. After he had lit the candle again, he saw there was jam on it. He had no explanation for that. He polished the cross on the seat of his trousers.

Strenehen started laughing. The laughter began to sound dangerous. It was swallowed up by deafening crashes. The stick of bombs had passed over his head. Somewhere it was ploughing up the earth. Stones hurtled from the sky, but none of them hit him. They thundered down on to the tin roof. The hurricane had crushed it. It lay on the ground like crumpled tinfoil. Strenehen sat down by the door. He was finished. His thoughts spun in a circle, his head was on fire, he rolled his eyes. There was soot everywhere. In his face, on his lips and in his mouth. He thought, I've been eating ashes.

He pressed his naked backside on to gravel. He put his hand down and picked up a handful of nails. He threw them weakly away, then looked at the door.

He giggled. '*Aren't you going to open up?*'

The door remained silent. He thought: I'll believe in God if it opens now. It doesn't have to be straight away, he thought. A minute. The door stood motionless. The metal was sweating. It formed droplets. Strenehen thought: God, God. If the door opens, he exists.

Half a minute passed. He thought: God's made up. And he spat. When no spittle formed, he gagged. Smoke came out of his stomach. Just smoke.

He stared at the door, saw the drops and felt thirsty. He stretched out his tongue and licked the metal. His tongue stuck there. The water was oil paint, blistered by the heat. His mouth was stuck together. He had to scrape off what was on his tongue. He used his fingernails. Then Jonathan Strenehen crept away. There was no point dying by this door. He could die anywhere.

'Dessy!'

Herr Cheovski waited for an answer. Firelight flickered across the walls. The heat grew more intense. When he looked at the window, he was like a hunted animal.

Nothing sprang to mind. He thought of his sons. He had forgotten their names. He tried to remember. Everything blurred together. The birth, the news, everything in between. Hours, days, years. 'Dessy, you've got to understand!' His speech quickened. 'I can't die. I beg you; you've got to remember.'

'What?'

'Life!' His voice grew shrill. 'I haven't lived yet. Fifty years. I've been living on hope for fifty years.'

She suddenly looked at him. 'And what have you been hoping for?'

'What for?' He had no answer. He exclaimed in a tearful voice: 'I can't die now just because my sons are dead.'

The flames crackled.

'Did they have to die?'

'Of course they did! You said we were paying the price.'

He looked at the glow of the flames on the walls and spoke even faster. 'You don't understand. God wills it. You do believe in God?' His voice was filled with doubt.

'No, I don't believe in God any more.' She tilted her head back and looked at the ceiling.

'That's bad.' He didn't know how to persuade her. 'That's bad,' he repeated, 'but come on now.' He reached for her hand. All he felt was unlimited fear. Gently she brushed his arm aside. 'Go on your own!'

'But . . . ?'

'Just go!'

While he was getting ready, he asked: 'You didn't really mean that?'

'Go on your own!'

'Dessy, come with me!' He stood in front of her. His eye went to the window. 'Will you forgive me?'

'Yes.'

'Dessy!' It was his last word. He leapt to the door. When he opened it, his body vanished in a cloud of smoke. She could no longer hear his footsteps through the crackling of the flames.

VIII

1892   *Hans Cheovski born.*

1911   *After Frau Geheimrat Wiesel preferred me to the other suitors, I am officially offered the hand of her daughter   sig. H.C.*

1913   *Dessy was twice invited to dance by His Excellency's adjutant. So my work is being acknowledged.   sig. H.C.*

1914   *Indescribable heroism, much of it on the part of simple people, on the occasion of His Majesty's visit. I have volunteered, but the office refused to give the necessary permission. sig. H.C.*

1915   *Rudolf is born. Dessy in good health. The doctor assures me everything is in excellent order.   sig. H.C.*

1917   *Walter born. The state of Dessy's health causes me concern. We are very short of good victuals. Not enough people in office.   sig. H.C.*

1919   *The city council confirms that I am to receive my old income and remain in the same position. Very serious financial losses.   sig. H.C.*

1932   *Rudolf passes his leaving examination with excellent*
         marks.   sig. *H.C.*

1933   *The lord mayor confirms me in office. My colleague Adler*
         commits suicide. Utterly incomprehensible. Dessy is quite
         depressed for several days.   sig. *H.C.*

1936   *Rudolf's desire is fulfilled at last. The 171st Infantry*
         Regiment accepts him as an ensign. Old traditional regi-
         ment. The uniform suits him. Everyone in the department
         congratulated me. Also, our work is now being generously
         supported by the Empire.   sig. *H.C.*

1939   *Walter and several colleagues called up. Everything very*
         optimistic, but Dessy is rather affected by the excitement. Of
         course we have to economise in the department now. I have
         temporarily dismissed some gentlemen.   sig. *H.C.*

1942   *Rudolf fell honourably in the field. Hand-written letter from*
         his commander. He was shot in the chest, and we must con-
         sole ourselves with the fact that at least he did not suffer.
         Dessy collapsed under the burden of the news. In addition,
         I have only temporary staff in the department.   sig. *H.C.*

1943   *Yesterday our 'Department of Monuments' was entirely*
         burned out.   sig. *H.C.*

1944   *Walter dead. Supposedly he did not suffer. So does God not*
         exist?   sig. *H.C.*

Through the walls it sounded like quiet thunder. The anti-aircraft gunner lay on the stretcher, and they stood around him. Four bare walls. White oil paint flaked off. It lay on the floor. Feet had trodden it. A fan hummed.

'A collapse,' said the doctor. 'What's his pulse like?'

'It's coming back.' The nurse knelt down. She opened the gunner's shirt. Over her shoulder the red-haired boy stared into the gunner's face. The beam from the light fell on his chin. His pimples glistened.

'When I opened the door he fainted,' a voice announced.

The boy explained quickly: 'And I caught him.'

He turned around. The voice belonged to a woman. She was standing in the doorway. Something glinted between her lips. A metal tooth. Grey hair hung over her forehead. She closed the door and confirmed: 'That's correct.'

'Silence!' The doctor reached into his white coat for his stethoscope. 'If I'm going to make an examination, I need silence,' he said. 'Absolute silence!' At that moment the gunner opened his mouth.

The doctor ordered: 'A glass of water and some bromide.'

'Yes sir,' answered the nurse.

The gunner opened his eyes. 'You've got to get up on the roof straight away!' He looked at the doctor. 'The gun commander, they've all been hit!'

His mouth and eyes closed again. His head fell to one side. He lay motionless. The fan hummed louder. It sounded like a swarm of hornets.

The woman asked: 'Is he dead?'

'No!' The nurse wiped a cloth over her brow.

'No!'

The boy called: 'I'm going with them, doctor!'

'Where to?'

'Up on the roof!' The boy put his hand on his chin. 'Up on the roof, doctor.'

'Registrar, you mean,' whispered the nurse.

'Just leave it!' The doctor shook his head. He turned towards the door. 'What business have you on the roof?'

'They're all wounded. You heard!'

'So?'

'So?' The boy looked beseechingly at the woman. Her metal tooth flashed. She nodded. The nurse stood up. No one said a word. Only the fan hummed.

'Bromide and water!' The doctor's voice sounded irritable.

'Straight away!'

The boy brought his heels together. They clicked. He lined up his hands with the seams of his trousers. 'Shall we go, Registrar?'

The doctor's face turned red. A vein throbbed at his temple. He asked: 'Are civilians giving orders to officers now?' He shouted: 'Get out of here, no one has any business here!'

The woman opened her mouth. She wanted to say something.

'Doctor!'

'Get out!' shouted the doctor. 'I won't have this. I can't have this!'

'Please.' The nurse was standing by the wall. A glass of water in her hand. Helplessly she held it out to him.

'Get out!'

'Come on, son.' The woman opened the door. She widened her mouth contemptuously. The metal tooth glinted like a nail.

The darkness was like a curtain. He had pushed up her skirt and was pulling at her underwear.

'Don't do it,' she whispered. 'Please, don't do it.'

'Oh yes!' His moist lips pressed against her neck. He sucked hard and dug his teeth into her skin. With his left arm he held her hands pinned to the stones behind her head. They were wrapped in the dark of the cave. Pebbles, rubble and what remained of a vault. It surrounded them like a suit of armour.

'Think of your daughter,' she begged. 'If your daughter was being . . .'

He wheezed. 'You aren't my daughter.'

She felt his fingers at her navel. Her panties tore. She struggled stubbornly against his knee, but he pressed her legs slowly apart. His body was half naked, its warmth invaded her. Nausea rose into her mouth.

'I've soiled myself,' she groaned. 'Can't you feel that I've soiled myself?'

'That doesn't matter.'

'You pig,' she cried. 'You pig!' She had to think of something. In a flash everything she knew darted through her. There was nothing to be done. It would happen in a second. In desperation she pulled her arm away. She ran her hand between their bodies. She touched him. She felt something sticky between her fingers, and he bit at her. She screamed. The pain in her neck was unbearable.

'Take your hand away!'

Automatically her arm moved back. There was nothing she could do.

His teeth began to loosen their grip, then the jolt ran through her abdomen. It burned like fire.

'Move!'

Everything mixed together: pain, nausea, repulsion. She stopped thinking. She began to whimper in time with their bodies. The panting of his lust in her ears, his heaviness on her. Stones pressed into her shoulders. The air smelled of excrement. She moved. He moved. Above her he gurgled like an animal.

'Here,' shouted one of the drunken soldiers, 'you see the whole world as a panopticon!' His rifle butt struck slats from the barrel. Wine splashed on the floor. 'Here you see the heroic death-struggle of a people, the sex-life of amoebas, a whore bathing, tram-tickets, cinema tickets and twenty empty barrels!'

'Silence!' roared the ensign.

'Schnapps is good for cholera!'

'Shut up!'

Rifle-butts and boots rang on the stones. The rabble got to their feet. They were swaying, but all standing.

'What did he loot?'

'Nothing,' said the corporal. 'He was just going to!'

The ensign's torso swayed back and forth. He stumbled towards a barrel and held on to it. His fingers clawed into the slats. He asked: 'What was he going to loot?'

'The station cash-desk,' explained the drunken voice.

'Fine!' The ensign laughed.

One of them asked: 'Will he be shot first, then hanged? Or the other way round?'

'Everything in its turn.' The ensign turned to the man. 'You admit you wanted to go to the station?' The man stood between the ensign and the soldiers. He stared at the ensign in silence. The walls and his face were the same colour.

'Talk, man!'

It rang out through the cellar. One of the soldiers spat. Spittle splashed on the wall.

'You bastard!' said the man.

'What?'

The man said: 'My wife was leaving with our child. The raid began, and they're at the station. I couldn't stand the uncertainty any longer. You'll never understand that!'

'Did you say bastard?' The ensign's glazed eyes started rolling. He looked at the ceiling.

'Yes!' The man heard the soldier's breath. He thought: This is the end.

'Me!' The ensign swayed again. He put his hand to his face. Beads of sweat ran over his temples. 'How old is your child?'

'Six!'

Dull booming penetrated the wall. Wine dripped on to the stones in the silence of the cellar.

'Me!' repeated the ensign. He covered his eyes with his hand. He brought his hand down. His face had changed.

'Three volunteers step forward!'

Suddenly behind the man's back the solid thud of sixteen boots rang out. Startled, he turned around. There they all stood. They had all stepped forward. Their eyes were red.

The ensign said: 'Forget what I said about three men. Let's all go to the station!' He bent for his belt. Immediately the soldiers put their helmets on.

The drunken voice called: 'He can wear mine.' Someone took the man by the hand and pulled him around. He didn't understand what was happening. There was a steel helmet on his head. Water was gushing from a tap. The ensign had turned it on. They held their faces under the stream. One of them opened the door. Dripping, with the man in the middle, they pushed their way out.

Gunpowder smoke wrapped them like cotton wool. The guns pounded. The ground trembled.

'For special valour!' The lieutenant reached under the prosthesis for the bag. 'I've been ordered to award you this!'

There was the crash of an explosion. He shouted: 'Congratulations! Wait for me by my bunker!'

'Yes, Lieutenant!'

The boy turned around. His shirt hung out of his trousers at the back. Thick smoke pushed its way between them. Lightning flashed. The lieutenant raised his arm, covered his eyes. Then he ran through a gap. In the smoke he came upon the next gunner.

'Halt!'

The boy put his hand to his helmet. 'Gunner Brink, K Five with the Mars gun, on the way to the basket stack.'

'For special valour.' He reached under his prosthesis into

the bag. He pulled out one of the crosses on its ribbon and hung it in the boy's buttonhole. 'I've been ordered to award you this.'

The boy quickly puffed out his chest. 'Thank you!'

'Congratulations. Go and wait for me outside my bunker.'

Smoke came towards them. Flames lit their faces. 'Yes, Lieutenant.'

The boy turned around. Stiff-backed, he walked straight into the clouds. He bore his pride through the noise, through the crashing and seething of a laundry where the washing was done with gunpowder. The lieutenant looked at the bag. Printed on it he saw grapes, a banana, two apples. Underneath was the inscription. But in the bag there were crosses.

He had had enough of crosses.

The lamps burned gloomily. A woman stood up. She said: 'I can't bear it any more.'

Three hundred people turned their heads. They were sitting on the benches, standing between them and leaning on the banisters of the stairs. The door was open. Fans hummed. The air was terrible. A child wept. The child was a floor above, and its weeping could be heard down below.

'Talk to one another,' a man advised. 'Silence makes people nervous.' He started whistling. Everyone listened to him and no one said a word. The man whistled tunelessly. When he had finished, someone clapped, and the woman pushed her way to the stairs.

A voice asked: 'Where are you trying to get to?'

'That's none of your business!'

'Stop!' There was movement. Someone grabbed the woman by the arm, led her back and sat her in her seat.

Three hundred people stared at the woman. Tears ran down her face. She sobbed silently.

'The worst thing is that you can't hear anything at all,' a voice whispered. 'It's like a coffin in here.'

'Then listen!' A woman laughed. 'I heard some pretty convincing bangs a few moments ago.'

A murmur of applause came from a corner and subsided again. A man's voice called: 'King beats jack. My go!' Playing cards fell on the floor. The man who had spoken bent down. There was whispering.

'Tell jokes!' a youth ordered. There was a suitcase in his lap. His shirt was open over his chest. 'A good joke,' he said.

'We,' someone called from the stairs, 'are winning the war!'

Everyone giggled, and the child from the upper floor stopped crying. When the laughter faded, someone spoke. 'Young man!'

'How can I help you?'

'I've been watching you the whole time. Doesn't it occur to you to stand up? Other people like sitting down, too!'

'Of course!'

The boy took his suitcase from his lap, reached under the bench, took out two crutches and swung on to them.

'I'm sorry,' said the voice.

'Nothing to be sorry about.' The boy smiled. 'If I get enough exercise, the regimental doctor says I'll live to be a hundred.' He sat down again. The crutches fell under the bench. A woman beside him reached into her bag and took out an apple.

'Take it.'

'Thanks.' The boy opened his suitcase. Inside it a plaster

model of a foot could be seen. He placed the apple beside it and closed the case again. The fans hummed.

In the seething smoke the leader of the unit ran like a machine from the flak tower.

He breathed in, pressed his lips together and closed his eyes.

He banged his head on a traffic sign. Stumbled. Fell off the pavement, arms spread wide, on to the road. Into the liquid asphalt.

It hissed. The tar was bubbling.

Tormented with pain, he rolled around like a black lump in the sticky mass.

He didn't scream, he didn't fight. His movements were dictated by the heat.

He was bent double, his head thrown high. His limbs were thrown apart as though he was embracing the earth.

He didn't look like a person any more, he looked like a crab.

He didn't die any manner of death that had ever been invented. He was grilled.

The woman with the metal tooth and the boy entered the empty air-lock. Everything smelled of smoke. His red hair gleamed in the lamplight. The fans hummed. He leaned against the barrel, and she stood by the door.

'Get away from there!'

The woman asked: 'Why?'

The boy bent over the barrel, dipped his face in it and straightened up again. 'Because I have to get on to the roof now!' Water ran from his nose, over his chin, the pimples. He looked as though he had been swimming.

'You're not climbing on to the roof.'

'Who says so?'

The woman said: 'I do.'

'They're wounded on the roof.'

'That's got nothing to do with you.' The woman put her hand on the bolt. 'You're not a doctor.'

'The doctor isn't going.'

'I know,' said the woman. 'I'm not deaf, you know.'

'They can't stop me!' The boy struck the barrel angrily. Water sprayed out.

The woman shrugged her shoulders. 'Try it.'

'Get away from the door.'

'I knew your mother before you were even born.'

'I know, you're the milk-woman.'

'From the corner,' added the woman.

The boy took a step forward. 'Let me out. I want to get to my comrades!'

'Comrades? Since when have you been a soldier?'

'You don't understand.'

The woman said: 'I understand more than you do.'

'How come?'

'Because I'm older than you.'

The boy smiled, embarrassed. He cautiously put one foot forward. He was wondering what part of her he should strike with his fist, her belly or her face.

'If you move an inch from where you are,' the woman said, 'I'll thump you on your stupid head so hard you'll think Christmas and Easter have come on the same day.'

The boy took two steps back out of embarrassment. His bottom bumped into the barrel. He looked at the metal tooth. It looked malicious.

'You've got to let me out!' he cried suddenly.

He ducked. His eyes flashed, then he jumped.

A blow landed on his cheek. His head flew to one side . . . He rubbed his chin. Without a word he went back to the barrel, leaned against the slats and studied the woman.

The hurricane was raging. Clouds of soot chased across the flames, pressing down on them and fanning them up again. Sergeant Strenehen felt his way through a ruined building. Collapsed walls surrounded him like the walls of a grotto. Fire roared behind them. He moved aimlessly. When the noise of an engine reached his ears he raised his head. '*Hello, guys?*'

He got no reply. He stared upwards anyway. What he saw was the sun. Its flaming disc stood in the middle of a square. His thoughts revolved around a ladder. Then he lowered his head again and saw shards of glass. He bent down and took off his shoes. He ran across, barefoot. You mustn't get dirty, he thought. The shoes dangled by their laces. He held the ends in his hand. When he had passed the shards he put his shoes back on. He didn't tie the laces. With his shirt open to the navel he stumbled forwards, legs spread. He walked bent over. His arms hung between his thighs. A brick flew past his face. It grazed his cheek.

'*What do you want?*' he asked. '*Are you trying to kill me?*' He giggled. He kicked at the brick with his left foot. His right foot stood on his shoelace and he fell headlong on the floor. He fell like a pillar. Cursing, he rose to his feet. Then he started to sing the national anthem. His voice croaked. Explosions drowned it out. All of a sudden he stopped.

He shouted in rhythm: '*One, two, three, four!*'

He marched.

Naked from the waist down. But getting nowhere. Sweat

broke from his pores. He wouldn't give in. He wanted to reach his goal. He bellowed as he marched towards the sun in the square.

He got a move on. Suddenly he gave up again. He staggered on through the rubble. It bothered him that the sun wasn't burning brightly enough. He wanted to light it. Climbing over a pile of stones he reached the street. Flames raged ahead of him. He raised his arm, fingers splayed. His tongue protruded from his mouth. Sergeant Jonathan Strenehen bared his teeth to the fire. A high-pitched giggle issued from his throat.

When his breath gave out, he ran away. He ran along the street, only thirty yards or so, until a new source of fire drew his attention.

The girl reared up and fell back. Stones pressed into her back. They were fighting with their bodies like enemies in the darkness. Suddenly he stopped.

'Let go of me!'

The girl stiffened. Nothing happened. Tears ran down her face. She was helpless.

'Leave me alone,' he said.

'But . . .'

'Whore!' He started roaring. 'Let go of me, you whore!'

'Yes!' she said. 'Yes! Yes!' But she couldn't. It was strange. 'Help!'

His roars were terrible.

They couldn't get out. Incendiaries were exploding in the street. The soldiers leaned against the walls of the passage, with the man in the middle. Children had scrawled something on the wall, a long time ago. The men covered it up with their bodies. The ensign stood at the entrance. Outside everything was on fire.

'Not a word!' The soldier who had recommended schnapps as a cure for cholera put his hand on the man's shoulder. 'If we can't do it by force,' he declared, 'we'll use reason.' His breath reeked of alcohol.

'Listen!' called the ensign. 'I need a volunteer. And it's urgent.'

'Me!' The soldier with the drunken voice raised his hand. 'I'm a witness. What's up?'

'A woman over there!' The ensign pointed over the road. 'She's standing at the window on the second floor, and the house is burning down. Fetch her down here, get her into the cellar.'

The soldier stepped forward. 'Yes, sir!'

'Your helmet!' called the man. 'Take your helmet with you!'

He put his hand to his head. Smoke poured into the corridor and enveloped him. He couldn't see anything now. His eyes were streaming.

By the time the smoke had passed, the soldier was already across the street. The ensign ordered: 'We will walk in single file. Keep close to the houses. Absolutely no running. Get ready!'

His last words were drowned by the crash of an explosion. He slung his submachine gun over his shoulder and stepped outside. At once he was forced to crouch down. Sparks sprayed into his face. The hurricane raged.

'I don't want any of you going soft on me!' he yelled into the entrance.

The man heard it. He thought: That's an order.

IX

I, Maria Sommer, born on 3 March 1891, had a dairy on the corner of Schmiedinger and Dammstrasse. My husband knocked out my third incisor on the right. He came to the military hospital on 7 August 1918 having been shot in the head, and was released on 24 December 1918 as an epileptic. They brought him to our apartment in a wheelchair, and a quarter of an hour later he was rolling about on the floor.

On 13 November 1928 he died in my arms of concussion, and I had loved him for twelve years. During all that time I was happy for three weeks, and that was the time before we got married. When we came home from church, his call-up papers were in the letter-box.

'Six men!'

The lieutenant slung the bag on to the table. The paper burst. A cross fell at the wireless operator's feet. 'Six men,' the lieutenant repeated. 'I've decorated them, the funeral can go ahead.'

The operator bent over. 'Do you want to go?'

'Yes.'

'But you don't have to?' The operator emerged from behind the table and put the cross back on top of it.

'No.'

The candle flickered. Its light shimmered on the walls, casting shadows. The lieutenant reached into his pocket, took out a cigarette, put it in his mouth. His shadow on the wall did the same.

'I'm ready.' The lieutenant spoke through gritted teeth. A bomb crashed outside. He listened. The guns went on firing.

He turned his back to the wall and lit the cigarette. His hand pointed to the table, to the crosses.

'Drugs for soldiers!'

He took the cigarette out of his mouth and dropped it. The tip of his boot flattened it out. The embers were extinguished on the ground. A spark flew. He said: 'But it's all part of it. They say some people need that kind of thing. The end justifies the means.'

'Always,' replied the operator and looked at the door.

Bombs whistled outside.

'I can refuse an order and go to the wall for it. But I can't give an order if I haven't the courage to carry it out myself,' the lieutenant declared.

The operator said: 'You don't have to explain anything to me.'

'Generals,' replied the lieutenant distractedly. 'Generals . . .'

'I'm not a general!'

The lieutenant said: 'Generals used to shoot themselves if they'd lost a battle . . .'

'Nowadays they'd write a book about it.'

'. . . We should bring that back.' The lieutenant turned towards the door. 'I've got to go.' All of a sudden he stopped. The floor shook beneath his feet. An earthquake was starting around the bunker. The walls rocked.

'Carpet bombing!' cried the operator. Startled, he ducked. The candle fell over.

'Under the table!' The crashing began. Blow after blow pounded down. He leapt towards the table. The concrete creaked.

'Now!'

The operator held his arms in front of his face. He crept under the table. All of a sudden the door came off its hinges and flew into the room. Dirt sprayed through the opening and rattled against the ceiling. There was smoke.

As suddenly as the crashing had begun, it stopped again. The earthquake, too, faded away. The operator got to his feet, knocking the table over. The crosses bounced on to the floor. He groped his way through the smoke to his equipment. He shouted into a mouthpiece: 'Sun, come in, please!'

A voice said: 'No casualties at Sun, ready to fire!'

'Moon, come in, please!'

'No casualties at Moon, ready to fire!'

The operator scratched his head. 'Jupiter, come in please!'

'Kiss me, we're still alive!' someone roared.

'Mars, come in, please!' said the operator.

An irritable voice exclaimed: 'Shut up with the stupid questions. Nothing at all has happened at our position!'

'No?'

The clouds were thinning. Daylight fell in through the doorway. It was starting to get dark. The operator's head emerged from the haze. He cried: 'No casualties, Lieutenant. No one's been hit, and they're firing again.' He sounded relieved.

'No one!' The lieutenant uttered the words like a scream. 'No one! Look!'

The operator turned around. He took two steps towards the door. A crater gaped outside it. The crater of a volcano. The earth was still steaming. Air glittered in the sun.

The lieutenant pointed outside with his prosthesis. 'They were lying there! They were lying there!'

'Who?'

'The six men!'

'Where?'

The lieutenant stepped through the opening. His voice babbled. 'I ordered them to.' He said in a normal voice, as though issuing a command: 'Lie down, wait here.'

'Where are you off to, Lieutenant?'

'The American! I've got to . . .' The lieutenant jumped on to the rampart of the crater. He ran along it.

'But!' The operator cried, 'Lieut—'

The lieutenant threw his arms in the air and looked at the ground beyond the rampart. He roared: 'Will you please announce yourselves?' Then he whispered to himself. 'I thought you were dead.'

The flames thundered in the street. The woman under the blanket clutched her chest. It was the theatrical gesture of someone fatally injured. She took another two tottering steps, and then sank down. Slowly on to her knees. She supported herself on the stones with one hand. She dropped her spade. She looked back over her shoulder, but there was no one behind her. She immediately straightened up again. The blanket slipped from her shoulders. She left it lying, jumped over a charred beam and ran diagonally across the road. On the way she brushed her helmet from her head. It rolled away. Her hair was blown about by the storm. She reached the other side and disappeared into a doorway. No one from the rescue party saw her. She was the last one.

Stones skipped down the steps, rolled in the darkness over the floor, through the control room.

The engineer said: 'Why don't you say something?'

'I have no reason to!' The mechanic ran the tip of his shoe

over the floor. It scratched. He sat on the rails. The copper was cold.

'Do you despise me?' asked the engineer.

'No.'

'I can feel it.'

'I don't despise anyone.' The mechanic spoke quietly. He kept hitting something against the door. Dull blows.

'There's fire up above us!'

'Yes.'

The engineer asked: 'Fancy some entertainment?'

'If it keeps you happy.'

'There's a Russian, a German and an American . . .'

'That's enough about Americans!' yelled the mechanic.

'Please yourself,' the engineer's voice said in the darkness. 'I just wanted to cheer you up.'

'I can take it or leave it.'

'Don't forget that I'm your boss.'

The mechanic whispered: 'I haven't forgotten. You've made it quite clear.'

'When?'

'That order you gave me, a little while ago.'

'Oh, yes!' answered the engineer. 'War needs men.'

The mechanic rose to his feet. His shoes squeaked. 'I want to tell you a story.'

'You can stay in your seat.'

The mechanic said: 'Once there were two men alone in a cellar.'

'Making it up?'

'No, it's true.' The mechanic stepped forward silently. He spoke slowly. 'The two men were standing in the dark, and one of them was one too many.'

'Do you hear it burning?' asked the engineer. The mechanic didn't reply.

'Do you hear it?'

'Yes.'

'What is actually burning?'

'The cable insulation!'

'Right,' said the engineer. 'When the raid's over we'll have to switch to low tension. That way nothing can happen.'

'Yes sir.'

The mechanic sat down again.

The ensign moved under the cover of the facade. He walked bent forward, keeping his right arm against the wall. His feet stumbled. As he went, he looked at the sky. His helmet was at the nape of his neck. He stopped at the nearest doorway. The squadron some miles above them was flying in V-formation. The tip of the V pointed along the street. He knew what that meant.

'Halt!'

He pushed the door open with his foot. The handle flew into the wall of the passageway. Plaster cracked from it. He stepped inside.

They came in one after the other, held their rifles in their hands and waited for the last man. The ensign counted them silently. Air pressure swept down the passage. Beyond the graveyard the guns roared. A plaque inscribed with names hung on the wall. The wall shook. The plaque kept rapping against it. The ensign read: Fischer, and, beside it, Wassermann. They lived on the first floor. A certain Blechschmid was a pensioner.

'Everyone into the cellar!' He turned around and ran on.

The floor was tiled. Their boots clattered. The paint on the walls was pale green. A door stood open at the end of the passage, and a voice rang out through their trampling footsteps: 'He won't go.'

The ensign stopped. 'What's up?'

'He won't go into the cellar.'

Two soldiers held the man firmly by his arms. He stood between them. His legs were braced against the floor and he leaned backwards. Drops of sweat ran down his nose. The other soldiers made way.

'You have to come with us,' cried the ensign, 'whether you want to or not.'

'But,' the man replied, 'you promised me I'd get to the station.' He panted.

'Yes. Alive, not as a corpse.' The ensign cried: 'Come on, get on with it!' His voice echoed. Fingers that felt like iron clamped around the man's wrists. They pulled him along. He stumbled forwards between the two soldiers. The freckled youth's face was at his side. Ahead of him the boots trampled down the stone steps. The ensign cried: 'I promise you we're just going to wait for them to fly past.' There was a dull rumble. A crash came from the street. Glass splinters flew through the passageway. The man would have fallen down the steps if the two soldiers hadn't been holding him. The warm air that rushed towards him smelled of bread. Warm bread.

Herr Cheovski sat on the steps. He was swathed in heat. He threw his arms in the air. 'Get back!'

'Why?'

'The house is on fire!'

'I noticed that.' The soldier dashed past him. He thought: What's he doing here? He ran up the stairs. He caught his boot and fell over. 'Damn!' He stumbled on. Smoke took his breath away. He thought: Save the woman! Heat came through a window. He jumped up. Doors burned. Air pressure had ripped them out. He leapt on. They lay in the corridors. He took three steps at once. Alcohol sweated through his pores. He wheezed. His rifle butt rattled along the banisters and got stuck between them. His breath whistled. He tore himself free. The second floor was untouched. He looked around. A door stood half open. He hadn't noticed it, and stumbled in. The woman must be in this apartment. He had a feeling about it. The corridor was full of smoke. He rubbed his eyes. Fumes gushed through the chinks of a door. He tore it open. A mirror exploded. The whole room was in flames. He slammed the door shut. The next one wouldn't open. He struck it with his rifle-butt. Something shattered. He walked through the frame and saw her. A chandelier lay on the table, smashed to pieces. The woman stood at the window.

'How may I help you?'

'Me?'

'How may I help you?'

He bellowed: 'Don't be frightened! I'll save you!'

With two bounds he was beside her. Behind him the door flew to one side. He grasped the woman around the hip and wrapped his arm around her. His rifle hung on his back. The butt broke a window-frame apart. The woman clasped her arm around his neck. She sobbed.

'No more tears!' His drunken voice. Her face was right in front of him. He wanted to be tender. 'Mum!' He whispered.

The woman hung passively at his chest. 'Mum!' He carefully pushed her through the opening. The rifle struck the door frame. He thought: Bloody drinking. If only I still had a mother. He carried the woman. His head was burning. He thought: Heat! How can I protect her against the heat? His hair and eyebrows were singed. 'Mum!' His hoarse voice trembled with rage.

A crash drowned his roars. The floor rose up, fell again. Stones crunched. The girl twitched.

'Aaaah,' the man gurgled. Suddenly he fell silent. But he wasn't dead. He did up his trousers with his hand. A fingernail scratched the girl's skin.

'Please!' she said. 'Please,' and felt him pulling back. She felt lighter. 'Please, stop now!'

'Whore!'

'Let me go!'

The man sneered: 'Of course.'

'Thank you!'

He snapped: 'Yes, thank me.'

'Thank you,' the girl repeated.

'You only talk when I tell you to,' the man ordered.

He rolled to the side. Something got caught in her dress. The fabric tore.

He asked: 'Why did you do that?

'What?'

The man cried menacingly: 'You!'

'I don't know!'

She opened her eyes, but she couldn't see anything. The darkness was impenetrable. Sand trickled down from above. It fell between her breasts. Brushed over her skin. A tender touch.

In the distance a storm roared through the rubble. The ground vibrated. The man paused for a moment, then grunted: 'You'll pay for that.'

He put his hand on her left thigh. His fingers pinched the flesh.

'Pity,' the girl whispered. 'Have pity on me, I'm bleeding.'

The man asked curiously: 'Where?'

'Between my legs.'

He ran his hand over her navel, felt his way down and touched her. 'That isn't blood,' he announced.

'I'm bleeding inside.'

'That's impossible.'

The girl answered quickly: 'But I can feel it.'

'You can feel it!' The man's hand moved back. 'What does it feel like?'

'It's flowing inside my belly.'

The man straightened. 'What do you mean, flowing? Is it warm?'

'Hot,' whispered the girl.

'Your imagination.'

'No!' the girl declared. 'It's running out, I can clearly feel it.'

'You!' The man clutched her face, her hair. He pulled on it.

'What?'

The man cried furiously: 'You can't die!'

He pulled her head to one side, as though to look at it. 'You can't!'

'But . . .'

'I don't want to be alone with a corpse,' said the man. 'I can't have that!'

'Die,' whispered the girl. 'Am I going to die?'

The man shouted, 'No!'

They dashed through the graveyard. A line of gunners. The lieutenant in the middle, three gunners to his right, three to his left. The sky was black. Not a trace of the parachutes. Only the graves were burning. They headed onwards. Trees like torches, crosses! Wreaths of ash. They ran ten paces. When the bombs whistled they hurled themselves to the ground, fingers clawing into the earth. They lay pressed to the ground. Their hearts pounded. Hammers on an anvil. They didn't dare breathe for terror.

I'm a murderer, thought the lieutenant. God loves murderers, too. Dear God, love me! The gunners weren't thinking about anything. One of them had a pound of shit between his legs. Two others let their breakfast coffee run into their trousers. The bombs struck, earth sprayed. The lieutenant jumped to his feet. The gunners were pulled in his wake. They ran through the splinters. All that sprayed down on them was dirt. The air boiled. They hurtled through it. There was more whistling. They lay there. There was a crash, and on they dashed again. A slit trench opened up ahead of them. They threw themselves into it. Everyone who jumped down jumped on a human being. They were bundles of rags, but not corpses. Frightened, they stumbled aside.

'It's nothing!' the lieutenant panted. 'Just Russians.'

The air was stuffy.

'A story!' the woman cried. 'I'll start.' She held a pot of chives under her arm. Light gleamed on her hair. The murmurs ceased. People started to jostle one another on the stairs. The mother with the crying child said into the silence: 'Quiet now, darling.' Fans hummed. A voice ordered: 'Off you go, then!'

'Silence!'

The child looked up, startled. The room grew quiet, and the woman with the chives said:

'Once there was a mental patient who was invited by some scholars to give them a talk. It was a . . .'

'That's good!'

'Silence!'

The woman went on: 'It was a scientific experiment, and the mental patient, still normal enough to be able to speak, acquitted himself of his task very eloquently, but without making any sense. Only at the conclusion did he become ambiguous, almost attaining the logic of a wise man. Gentlemen, he said, my remarks are at an end. After all that you have heard you will think me a fool. But are you sure?'

Someone giggled.

'Sadly I am only one man, while you are many. Always reflect how easily that might change on a whim of nature. People like myself would populate the earth. You, however, would form that hopeless minority. Do you know what would happen then?'

The woman took her chives out from under her arm and put them between her legs. She went on: 'With this question the speaker brought his address to a close, stepped from the podium with a modest gesture and sat back down upon his chair. Beside his chair stood his warder.'

The woman fell silent, and the fans hummed.

'Is that it?'

'Yes.'

'But,' someone called, 'we're not in the minority!'

Everyone laughed. Whistles rang out on the stairs. They came from the loudspeaker.

'Silence!'

The laughter ceased. Two hundred and seventy heads turned towards the door.

A melodious voice sounded from the loudspeaker. 'Enemy activity continues in the north and west of our country. Air battles over the suburbs. A new formation on its way. Over!'

The fans hummed. The child began to cry. One of the light-bulbs went out. Shadows deepened.

Someone asked: 'Who's had the fire on in here?'

The voice sounded furious. Boots trampled on stones. The door opened. A beam of light shone out and the soldiers jostled their way in. It was a bakery.

'Oh!' cried the corporal. 'How cosy!'

Three iron steps led down from a little platform. The light-bulb on the ceiling illuminated everything. Bare tables, flour-dust, the utensils and a figure by a bucket.

'Hello!' The ensign moved his submachine gun from his left hand to his right. The figure by the bucket turned around. Dough bulged from its mouth, stuck to its hands, dripped from its chin on to its chest. The figure didn't say a word. Its eyes stared at the soldiers. They bolted the door.

'Hello!' The ensign laughed hoarsely. The safety catch clicked on a rifle. Rumbles penetrated the walls. They were explosions. They were coming closer. Everyone began to wait.

The ensign pointed to the bucket. 'You *rabotnik* – you worker?'

The figure gave no answer. Its head was shaven. It was not wearing a uniform. It was dressed in rags.

'He isn't working,' said the lance corporal, 'he's looting!'

Bombs crashed in the street. Flour-dust came from the ceiling. It floated down. On to the tables, on to the utensils and the figure. The light began to flicker. Shadows flitted across the walls. Everything started to shake. The figure, the soldiers, the little platform and the walls.

The ensign asked: 'What you do?'

'The fellow's eating sourdough,' a voice explained.

Someone giggled. The figure stood motionless. The light fell on a hollow-cheeked face. It vanished. The floor tilted as though on a ship. It rose again. A cane fell over. It skittered over the stones. Slipped into a corner.

'Let's play court martial,' a soldier whispered. It was supposed to be a joke. No one laughed. The ensign climbed down the steps. He ordered: 'Go into the corridor, I'm going to . . .' An explosion crashed. He finished: 'do him in.'

His gun gave a metallic clank. He cocked the bolt. The soldiers by the door turned around. They filed out of the bakery. In their midst was a man in civilian clothes. Someone grumbled. The last one out closed the door. The bombs were constantly falling.

'*Vri tot stena* – over to the wall!' ordered the ensign.

The figure stayed where it was. A piece of dough fell off its chest and on to the floor. In the shadow the ensign saw two feet. The shoe-leather gaped. Toes protruded from the shreds. He repeated: '*Vri tot stena*!' His voice sounded sarcastic. The power failed. The lamp went on glimmering faintly. The figure became a black outline. It moved and went to the wall. A couple of feet before it reached the wall it turned around. It raised its head and stared at the lamp. A storm was raging in the street. It thundered on and on.

'Turn around!' The ensign's hands were sweating. He raised his submachine gun to his hip. The outline shook its head.

'Fine!' The ensign put the butt to his shoulder. He slowly raised the muzzle from below, and all of a sudden he fired. Bullets rattled into the walls. Mortar sprayed. A ricochet twanged. It sounded like a violin-string breaking.

'You kaputt!'

The ensign took the gun from his shoulder. Then he pointed underneath a table. The lamp flickered, became bright again. He looked at the figure. It didn't move. He ordered impatiently: 'Go on, go on!'

'You shoot me!' The figure raised its arm, pushed the sleeve back, showed purulent tissue. It was festering from the wrist to the elbow. 'You shoot me!' The figure let its arm drop. With its left hand it opened its shirt. Its nipples were covered with black hair.

'*Nix verstehen*?' asked the ensign.

'I understand!' The figure looked towards the bucket, at the traces of dough. The lamp-beam cast circles around the room. The walls trembled. One of the figure's hands rose up and pointed at its hairy chest.

'Bang, bang! Please!' said the figure.

The ensign shook his head. '*Nyet!*'

'Please!'

'*Nyet!*'

The light grew fainter again. The walls were covered with

shadows. The voice came from the darkness. 'Bang, bang! Please, please!' At that he swung the submachine gun around and fired from the hip. Bullets sprayed. A scream echoed through the burst of fire, then the figure emerged from the darkness. It took two steps forward, turned on its axis and fell to the floor. Blood dripped from its neck. It mingled with the flour-dust.

The ensign turned around and walked through the bakery. He stumbled over the cane and pushed it aside. He climbed the three steps up and opened the door.

'He's dead,' said a voice.

The ensign looked at the floor. He was blinded by darkness. He couldn't see a thing. 'Of course.'

'I don't mean the Russian,' said the voice. '*He* is dead.'

The soldiers stood by the walls. Their weapons clanked.

The ensign screamed: 'That's impossible!'

'No, it all happened too fast!'

'Yes sir!' The lance corporal explained. 'He suddenly rushed up the stairs. We followed him. He jumps through the hallway, gets to the street. A splinter tears open his forehead. From his temple to his mouth.' The lance corporal paused.

'But . . .'

'What do you mean, but?'

'He died painlessly.'

'Is that all?'

'Yes.' The lance corporal cleared his throat. 'I'm sure it's all for the best, his child's probably dead, after all.'

'Shit. I can't leave you alone for a minute without something happening,' answered the ensign. 'Where is he?'

'In the hallway.'

'And?'

The soldier with the freckles said: 'And? Isn't that enough? I suggest we get out of here.'

'Where to?'

A voice called: 'The flak tower.'

X

I, Heinrich Wieninger, lieutenant in an anti-aircraft unit, born on 9 September 1911, trained as a cook and was due to take over our hotel on my father's 65th birthday. At the age of seven I was cutting onions with my right hand. At the age of twenty I was stroking a girl's bare shoulder with my right hand. Three years ago I used the same hand to cut off a dead man's legs.

He was lying in the snow, he had frozen to death and he owned a pair of fur boots. I couldn't thaw out the whole body, so I took the boots with the chopped-off legs and put them in our dug-out. When they warmed up, the legs fell out. It was very easy.

Two years later I put my trousers on with a hand made out of papier mâché. When I was drunk I used to beat it on the table. If I live another ten years I will stand in the lobby of a hotel. I will nod my head to the guests. On my right side hangs a hand made of papier mâché. No one will ask me where my real flesh-and-blood hand is. Who cares about that? I do!

The lieutenant ducked. Earth sprayed over his head. One of the Russians stumbled towards him and threw himself down. He folded his hands.

'Lower your rifles!'

The lieutenant turned around and shouted: 'Can't you see they're terrified!'

The gunners squatted in the trench, the muzzles of their weapons pointing at the Russians. They put their guns on the ground. 'You seen Americans?' roared the lieutenant. He lifted his prosthesis towards the sky. Pointed into the smoke. The Russian on the ground turned his head. The others came hesitantly forwards. But the lieutenant got no answer. The skin of their faces was like leather.

'Airmen!'

The lieutenant spread his arms. He walked among them, mimicking somebody floating. The figures immediately flinched. When he smiled at the Russian in front, the man showed his teeth. He was as wary as an animal.

'Nothing!'

The lieutenant shrugged his shoulders. 'Nothing?'

He reached into his pocket, took out cigarettes and threw them to the men. They didn't bend down. Only the Russian on the ground stood up. He pointed over the trench. Bombs whistled.

'Two kaputt!' he shouted. 'One not kaputt!'

'Americans?'

A fountain of stones sprayed into the sky. A shock wave swept across the ground. The Russian and the lieutenant collided, then ducked. Earth showered from the sky. When they stood up, they held out their hands to each other. One of the gunners picked up his rifle.

'It's nothing,' said the lieutenant. He quickly removed the arm with the prosthesis from the Russian's hand, and the gunner lowered the muzzle of his rifle.

'Americans?'

The Russian shrugged. He spat. His head waggled. He had sacks wrapped around his feet. When the lieutenant looked over the trench he saw a crater. A bare leg lay on the edge. It was torn off above the knee. Its calf was covered with ulcers. 'He's not American,' he said, confused.

'Comrade!' The Russian nodded. 'Good comrade!'

'Yes!' The lieutenant turned irritably towards him. A gunner stood in the trench, legs splayed. With his trousers open, he reached between his legs. His hand fished out shit and smeared it on the wall of the trench.

'Christ in heaven!' the lieutenant yelled. 'You pig, at least preserve your human dignity!' A face looked at him, distorted with fear. Uncomprehending. Then he roared: 'Come on, quick march! Forwards!'

He was the first to obey his own command.

★

The water was evaporating from the ground. The air-lock was filled with haze. The woman with the metal tooth stood at the door. She didn't move. Black woollen socks reached to the hem of her skirt. A piece of her petticoat peeped out. It was torn.

'If there was an officer in the bunker,' the boy whispered, 'I could report him.' He glanced over his shoulder at the door of the sickbay.

The woman folded her hands. She was standing in the gloom.

'Who?'

'The doctor, of course.'

'And me?'

'They don't hang dairywomen,' the boy replied. He poked his finger into his nose. All of a sudden he hastily scratched his pimples like a monkey. A trickle of blood ran down his chin. He wiped it away.

'You don't really believe,' the woman asked, 'that they'd hang him, just because he wouldn't go on to the roof?'

'Of course they would!' The boy declared magnanimously: 'It's only fair and just! The gunners are dying, after all.'

'Justice.' The woman screwed up her mouth.

'In the old days they quartered them.'

The boy stepped over to the barrel. He reached his hand into the water and splashed a wave against the slats. It sprayed out. His hand moved slowly back and then forwards again. Haze from the walls settled on his face. It glistened. With each movement he whispered: 'Hang him! Hang him! Hang him!'

'Be quiet!'

'Hang him!'

The woman shouted: 'Shut up!'

'If it bothers you!' The boy drew his hand out of the barrel. He wiped it on his trousers. He shrugged his shoulders. 'There's a war on, after all.'

The fans hummed.

'You don't have to tell me that there's a war on. I know that myself!'

'Even more will be hanged after the war.' The boy reached for the barrel again. Gratified, he nodded his head.

'Who?'

'The losers! Who did you think? It's in all the history books. Have you never noticed?' He laughed knowingly.

'Where's your sister, by the way?' the woman asked suddenly.

'On her way to the station.'

'What?'

'I hope she won't get all smashed to pieces,' the boy answered thoughtfully. 'There's a lot of metal in the air.' He puffed out his chest and adopted a frosty expression.

Steps led out of the smoke. Boots could be seen. Something black pushed its way out. Burning wood flew through the air. It exploded on the tiles.

'Grab her!' gasped a voice. 'I can't go on.'

Herr Cheovski leaned against the wall. His trousers were torn. He was trembling. His eyes were watering. 'That's my wife.' He stepped forward and reached towards a bundle.

'Careful!'

The soldier knelt and sat down on the last step. The figure lay motionless between his legs. Over its head hung a combat jacket. The soldier was in his shirt-sleeves. The material was singed. His arms were covered in blisters. 'Carry the woman into the cellar,' he groaned. 'I can't go on.'

'Dessy!' cried Herr Cheovski. 'Come on, Dessy!'

'Are you related?' The soldier looked up. His face was blue. Where others have hair, he had ashes. On the top of his head, above his eyes, on his lips. There was no skin left on his face. His cheeks consisted of burned flesh. He wheezed: 'Quick, man, save her!'

Herr Cheovski wrapped his arms around his wife. 'Of course, of course!' He babbled senselessly. He took the body in his arms, turned around and tottered off with her. The combat jacket dragged along the ground. They both disappeared into the smoke.

The soldier watched after them. When he could no longer see them, he reached behind him. His rifle lay on the steps. His muscles were cramped with pain. He clenched his teeth. Fire was all about him. In his brain, before his eyes, under his skin. He screamed.

The wind whistled. The barrels of the anti-aircraft gun pointed at the platform. Smoke raced through the struts of the gun-mounting. It forced its way through, as persistent as poison gas.

Sunbeams fell on the concrete. The four figures lay on their bellies. Their bodies stuck to the smooth ground. One of them lay still, his arms outstretched. His right hand held a white cloth. He lay there as though he wanted to give himself up. The gun commander held the loader by the hand. Beneath them the concrete had discoloured. Sweat ran down their temples. They were lying in the desert. A hot storm swept over an infinitely smooth surface. The ropes they hung

from stretched above them. One rope flapped over the edge of
the platform. The earth around their island burned, and a
storm was raging. Each new impact moved their bodies.
Quakes ran through them like electric shocks. Burning paper
sailed through the air. Splinters crashed against stones. Shrill
sounds. Birds from the primordial world. They hissed, spite-
ful as reptiles.

A hundred and fifty feet away boards leapt into the air.
Destruction ran riot.

Bombs were being dropped.

The girl whimpered quietly. The man lay next to her and listened. He couldn't see her, but he could feel her. The wall
groaned. He heard it creak. Sand trickled ceaselessly. It fell
into the abyss. No beginning and no end.

The man murmured: 'How do you feel?'

'I feel hot.'

'So do I,' said the man. He peered into the darkness. His
shirt clung to his back. He lay jammed between her body and
rubble. Something pressed against his hip. An iron bar.
'Listen,' he said.

There was a gurgling sound.

'That's me,' said the girl. 'Inside.'

He whispered: 'Can you still feel it?'

'Yes.'

'It'll pass.' He said loudly: 'I'm sure it'll pass.'

They said nothing.

One stone broke away. It rattled against other stones. A
scratching noise came out of the silence.

'Something's running down my leg,' said the girl.

'Blood?'

'No, an animal.'

'That'll be cockroaches,' the man explained. 'Do you want me to look for them?'

'Please don't.'

The gurgling sound came again. Suddenly water splashed from the ceiling. Not that much. It sprayed between their bodies.

'What is it?'

'Water!'

'We're drowning!'

'No.'

The girl asked: 'Can't you help me? I'm frightened.'

'Help you how?'

'The blood,' the girl whispered. 'I'm bleeding.'

A tremor ran through the earth. A long way off an explosion roared.

The man cried: 'You should stand up.'

'I can't.'

'Sit up, then.'

Two hands ran over the girl's neck. They reached behind her back and pulled her up. Her forehead struck some masonry. She said: 'It's no good.' The hands let go, and she lay back down again.

'Knock!' she ordered.

'What?'

'Knock, they're bound to hear us!'

The man felt his way along the ground. His fingers found a piece of brick. He used it to strike the iron by his hip. It was a pipe. He could tell from the sound it made. Gravel fell from the rubble.

He said: 'It's no good!'

'Please, knock!'

'They won't hear us during the raid,' the man explained.

'There is no raid.'

'But listen!'

The girl listened. A faint hum passed through the stones.

'Can you hear it?'

'Yes,' said the girl. 'But I don't want to die.'

The man laughed.

'If you knock,' the girl said, 'I won't say a word about what happened.'

'I'm not going to knock.'

'Please!'

'No!' The man grunted. 'No one's going to find us. We're going to suffocate or starve here. I'd be better off killing myself.'

He rolled to one side. His hand searched around in the darkness. He felt his way along the rubble, the girl's forehead, then his own body.

An angel spread out its arms to bless them. One wing was missing. It was made of marble. They dragged the boy past it.

He scraped along the earth on his back. The lieutenant was pulling his right arm, one of the gunners his left, and the others were running after them. There was a chapel on the way, and they stumbled in with him. It was a monument.

'Lay him on the slab,' ordered the lieutenant. He took a pack of bandages from his pocket, as they lifted him up. An inscription announced: Here lies . . . The wounded man covered it with his body. Mortar from the wall sprayed on to his face. The walls swayed. An urn fell over. It burst into pieces on the ground. Ash was blown away like dust. A howling noise surrounded the chapel. Shrill whistles rang out.

Something exploded outside, against the wall. It broke apart, with a singing noise. The lieutenant looked up. The roof was missing. The wing of a bomber glittered in the sunshine. He shouted: 'Pull off his trousers!'

'Yes sir!' They were screaming, too.

Bombs burst like huge balloons of explosive gas. The air pressure swept past the entrance, tearing flowers along with it. A wreath rolled past. The brass laurel wreath.

'Unroll the dressing!' yelled the lieutenant. A hand reached for the bandage roll and tore it open. Suddenly everything was quiet. Silence! The lieutenant breathed out.

'Write,' whispered the wounded man, 'to my mother that I've got the First Class.'

'You can't . . .' A shadow. A phosphorus canister burst apart before the altar. 'Speak!' yelled the lieutenant. There was fire before his eyes. The walls burned. His prosthesis hissed. It was on fire. He broke it off against the slab. He pulled it off. A man was rolling on the floor, in the crackling phosphorus. Flesh crackled. On the slab lay the wounded man's trousers. The lieutenant fell to the floor with them. Shit flew out. Sizzled in the heat. The trousers burned. The stench of urine permeated everything. The lieutenant yelled: 'Get out of here! Get out!'

He leapt to the entrance. Four gunners were standing outside. Two were burning to death behind him.

'Lieutenant!' they yelled. 'Lieutenant!' One of them was weeping. 'Lieutenant!' The Iron Crosses dangled at their chests.

'Get back!' he roared at them. 'To the emplacement!'

The bonfire was behind him.

*

'For heaven's sake,' a man announced. 'We'll make them pay for this!'

The fans hummed. The people on the stairs turned around. Downstairs a door banged. Someone cleared his throat.

'With all the means at our disposal,' a woman agreed.

The lamps cast circles over their heads. Some of them moved. A shoe scraped on concrete. The door banged again. Whispering started in a corner.

'It's only human,' a singsong voice asserted.

'I can imagine!'

The loudspeaker on the stairs emitted a whistle. Immediately they all fell silent. But when nothing else happened they went on talking.

A man said loudly: 'From the constructive point of view, it's only the centre of a triangle. Divide up the cone. The product is abstract.'

'Quite correct.'

'Of course the concept is symbolic.'

'That's my opinion exactly.'

Suddenly everyone was talking at once. Someone whistled. A woman declared: 'Smoke poisoning is incurable in cats.'

'Yesterday!' two men said at the same time, and a voice called: 'If my daughter had died a normal death, I'd still believe in God today.'

The conversations swelled. A quiet drone came from the walls. In a moment they all fell silent. Three hundred people breathed in unison.

XI

I, Jonathan Strenehen, born on February 8 1918, helped my parents to run the gas station they own on the highway from Fort Worth to Dallas.

On Sundays I took the old Ford and drove Mary up to the lake behind the hills. A little toy bear dangled above the windscreen on elastic. If I wanted to kiss Mary, I first used to shove it behind the sun-shield. The little teddy was always very curious. Sometimes he fell out and startled Mary. She liked wearing clothes with wide straps. At the lake we drew the ground-plan of our future house in the sand or dreamed about other things.

In the afternoon we heard dad's rifle going off when he was shooting birds. Once he watched us through his telescope. He stood in the reeds for half an hour, not moving a muscle. We acted as though we couldn't see him, and he finally got bored.

On Sunday evenings mom invited Mary for dinner. In the summer we also got banana ice cream from Bardly. Dad roasted his catch on the open fire by the veranda. While Mary helped lay the table, I lay on the couch winking at her, and we were already looking forward to our trip back to Mary's parents in the Ford.

The rifle-butt struck the tiles. The soldier crept to the wall from the stairs. There was smoke everywhere. The staircase collapsed with a crash. A glowing wooden beam came down and landed by the soldier's feet. Sparks danced down the passageway like glow-worms. The soldier groaned. He slid along the floor on all fours, pulling his weapon behind him by its strap. Glass splinters stabbed into his palms. The pain was unbearable. His head seemed to inflate. He crept towards the steps. A flight of stone stairs led into an abyss. He supported himself on his hands and sank down again.

He hung his torso over the steps and slipped down head-first. Darkness came over him. His knees struck edges. His rifle clanked after him. The abyss yawned. He slipped faster, slid over a flat patch and suddenly struck the wall. He lay where he fell on his left side.

'Help me,' he whimpered. 'Someone help me!'

The stench of scorched leather spread around him. 'Please help me!'

He wailed through the darkness. The outline of a figure came up to him. He heard the clanking of a metal bucket.

Suddenly someone poured water over him. It splashed, then hissed. His shirt fell apart like tinder. Blisters burst on his arms. Steam formed over his head. With a scream he pulled his rifle to him. The strap swung through the air. He put the muzzle in his mouth. Steel struck his teeth. His right hand felt for the trigger. His index finger bent. No. The safety catch was on. Trembling, he twisted it back. The sights cut into his jaw like a knife. He reached for the trigger again. And pushed it back.

The nurse stood with her back to the stretcher by the wall. She was holding her glass of water in her hand. The doctor was leaning against the door. He was smoking. The gunner sat on a chair. His arms hung down. He stared at the floor.

'Stand up!'

The gunner staggered to his feet. His helmet lay beside the chair. Hair stuck to his forehead. Dazzled by the light, he looked away.

'Put your helmet on!'

The gunner bent down and put the helmet on his head. He pulled the strap over his chin. Shadows fell over his eyes. He let his arms dangle. His fists were clenched.

'Attention!'

The gunner's heels clicked together. His fists opened. He pressed his hands to his trousers, drew in his chin and looked straight ahead. A cloud of smoke from the doctor's cigarette drifted past his face. It entered the vortex of the fans and vanished like a ghost into a hole in the wall.

'Just so you know. I have no time for soldiers who can't keep their heads.'

The doctor puffed on his cigarette. Smoke rings floated to the ceiling. They dispersed without a trace.

'Pull yourself together. It's up to you whether I report you or not.'

'Sir . . .'

'Shut up!'

The nurse turned around. She said: 'He's had a collapse.' Her hands were trembling. She pressed her glass of water to her chest. A brooch flashed. Glass stones on clover-leaves.

'Who had the collapse, you or him?'

'Doctor!' The glass fell from the nurse's hand. Shards sprayed. She opened a box on the wall, took out a packet, walked to the door. The light from the lamp fell on her face. It was powdered. She was wearing lipstick. The door flew open and crashed shut again. The doctor was alone with the gunner. He shook his head.

'Do knee-bends.'

The gunner didn't move.

'I told you to do knee-bends!'

The gunner stretched his arms out, bent his legs and stood up. He was about to bring his arms down.

'Go on!'

Again the gunner raised his arms and bent his legs.

'Faster!'

The gunner stood up, bent his knees. Immediately sweat ran over his face. He gasped.

'Stop!'

Arms outstretched, the gunner cowered in a balancing position.

'Are you going do that another fifty times or go straight up on to the roof?'

'Yes, sir!'

'What does that mean? Clear off!'

'I'm going straight away.'

The gunner stood up. He clicked his boot-heels together and put his hand to his helmet. 'Yes, sir!'

He turned around on his right heel and stumbled. When he was standing in the doorway, a belt flew at his back.

'Do you always forget your uniform?'

Behind the gunner, the doctor was stretching. He looked at his watch. The second-hand ran tirelessly over the watch-face.

Once outside, the gunner didn't walk into the air-lock. He walked down the stairs to the cellar. Down below he lay on one of the stretchers. His neighbour was twelve-year-old human flesh.

An orderly's voice said: 'I'm amazed the old man sent you down here.'

Sergeant Strenehen was looking at a concrete house. It had no windows. It rose into the sky like a monument. There were slits in the walls. But it didn't keep anyone out. That was a miracle.

Strenehen giggled. He picked up a brick and threw it against the stone. The brick exploded. It lay in the smoke.

'. . . *the door!*' yelled Strenehen.

He thought: All houses have doors. If it hasn't got a door it isn't a house. If it isn't a house it doesn't need a door.

Splinters whirred over his head. He ducked slowly and lost his balance. Stumbled like a drunk. Then he sat down and bared his teeth. Suddenly he started to weep. A tear ran from his cheek down his throat to his chest, which rose and fell with his sobs. The storm ruffled his hair. Strenehen wept bitterly. He crouched, lonely, in hell.

★

Damp air rose up. Water ran down the air-lock walls. The puddles on the floor got bigger. The boy wiped his nose with his arm. He got snot on his sleeve. He was rubbing it into the material with the balls of his hands when the door from the corridor opened, and the nurse walked in.

She said: 'Have you got a helmet there?'

'Why are you crying?' replied the woman with the metal tooth. The boy turned round. The humming of the fans intensified. They sucked in the warm air.

'I'm not crying!' The nurse's eyes glittered. 'I need a helmet.' She held a box under her arm. Her eye fell on the boy. The woman at the door pulled her lips up. Her tooth flashed. 'For the registrar?'

'No, for me.'

'Ah.'

'Please.'

'We haven't got any helmets,' said the woman.

'Then that's . . .' The nurse walked quickly to the door and put her hand on the handle. 'Then that's how it'll have to be.'

'Not necessarily.' The woman pushed the nurse's arm away. Her arm fell to her side, and the nurse turned her head in surprise. Her lipstick was smeared.

'Do you want to get out?' asked the woman.

'Of course!'

'You can't.'

'Why?'

'Because I'm standing in the doorway.' The woman smiled.

'I'm Countess Baudin. I have to get on to the roof to tend to the wounded. Open the door!'

The boy whispered suddenly: 'I'll go with you, sister.'

'Pleased to meet you,' said the woman. 'My name is Sommer. I can't open the door.' She looked up at the ceiling and declared: 'Anyone can come in here, but only one person gets out.'

'That's enough.'

The boy whispered: 'The old bag's gone mad, sister.'

'Listen, young fellow!' The tooth flashed between the woman's lips.

The sister said: 'I'm begging you!' She tilted her head, waiting, but no answer came. She waited.

'Get back to your doctor!'

'My dear woman!'

The woman spread her legs and braced her arms on her hips. 'My lady!'

The boy whispered: 'Cow.'

'I just want you to know this!' the nurse shouted. 'The soldiers on the roof are bleeding to death.'

'Did the doctor order you to go up there?'

'No.'

The woman shouted: 'Go back into the dressing station.' Something fizzled in her mouth. Fine spittle sprayed on the nurse's nose.

'Careful!' yelled the boy. He jumped out from behind the barrel, but the woman looked at him sharply and he stopped in his tracks.

'Here!' The nurse put her hand to her chest, opened a brooch, pulled it off and held it out to the woman.

'Take that!' she said hastily. 'They're real stones!'

'How long have you been doing this?' The woman looked contemptuously at the brooch.

'Today's my first shift.'

'And then after that you'll be going back.'

The boy cried reproachfully: 'She even hit me!'

'Listen,' said the nurse. 'It doesn't matter about me. My husband isn't alive. Our son is missing. Let me up there.'

'If your boy is missing, you must wait for him.'

'No!'

'Yes!'

The nurse said: 'He was a sailor.'

'Even so.'

'Sister!' cried the boy. 'Between us we can take care of her.'

'Now hold on,' answered the woman.

The nurse's face suddenly crumpled. She sobbed, and at once the woman put her arm around her shoulders. She said quietly: 'Come on, tell me. I understand. I understand everything.' She led the nurse away from the door to the wall. The boy opened his eyes wide. His mouth started opening. He forgot there was no one guarding the door. He ran his hand excitedly over his pimples. He was about to hear a hero's tale. That was just what he wanted.

The man in civilian clothes lay in the corridor. Face turned to the ground. Legs splayed.

A trail of blood ran over the tiles. Drops, like a bird's footprints. A smell of gunpowder hung in the air. The air was seething beyond the door. The soldiers stood along the walls. Two parallel rows. The passage ran between.

'Let's go back to the bakery!' urged the lance corporal. He looked at the ensign. 'Better to wait there than die on the way, and we're not going to miss anything.'

A voice groaned: 'My head's buzzing.'

'Let's go to the bakery!' someone shouted.

'Halt!'

The ensign took his submachine gun from his shoulder and put it to his hip. 'Stop this chattering. You wanted to go to the bunker. Now we're going.'

'I wasn't thinking!' called a voice.

'What?'

The ensign stepped from the wall into the middle of the corridor and stood with his face to the doorway. His boot touched the dead man's left hand. He snatched his foot back.

The voice explained rather more quietly: 'What I said about the bunker. I thought the raid was over.'

'That's right, sir,' the soldier with the freckles confirmed eagerly.

'We all had the same idea.'

A rifle-barrel clanked. Smoke snaked over the tiles.

'No!'

A razor-sharp voice said irritably: 'We were all involved in that nonsense with the man. That's enough of that. We've sobered up now.'

All heads turned to the dead man. They did so with machine-like precision, and the ensign slowly took three steps back. When the soldiers looked up again they were staring into the muzzle of his gun.

One of them stretched. He asked: 'What's going on?'

'We're going to the bunker.'

'No!'

A creaking came from the stairs. The wood was warping in the heat.

The ensign took another step back. 'Who's in charge here? Me or you?' They all looked at him.

A slab of plaster came away from the wall and slapped on the tiles.

'Lutz!' The lance corporal cleared his throat. 'We've always stuck together. Don't do anything stupid now.'

The gun-barrel clanked again. The ensign thumbed back the safety catch of his submachine gun.

'Anyone else who moves an inch,' said the lance corporal, 'will get a clout from me personally.'

Glass splintered in the street.

'My opinion entirely,' observed the soldier whose head was buzzing.

'Lutz,' asked the lance corporal, 'why don't you want to go back to the bakery?'

The ensign looked at his gun.

'Tell us!'

'Because of the dead Ivan!'

The soldier with the rifle answered: 'You were the one who killed him, not us!'

'We killed him together.'

'Nonsense.'

'Stop talking,' called the soldier with the freckles. 'Let's go to the bunker.' He took a step forward, hesitated and looked at the ensign.

The lance corporal reached for his helmet with both hands.

He straightened it. 'You go ahead, Lutz.'

The ensign didn't move.

The lance corporal said: 'I want you to go ahead.'

'Five paces apart!' The ensign carefully uncocked his

submachine gun. He turned back the safety-catch. 'You walk behind me. It's only three hundred yards.'

He walked forwards through the rows of the soldiers, and they followed him.

The fans hummed evenly. A crunching noise came from the wall. Three hundred people held their breath. The crunching stilled. Three hundred people breathed out. A draught blew through them.

A woman said: 'Our district's for it now.'

The boy with the crutch took his suitcase off his lap. He put it between his legs. A fly buzzed about beside the door. It flew in circles. Its shadow flitted across the wall. A black dot. Suddenly it collided with the ceiling and reeled to the floor. A bench creaked.

'There's an anti-aircraft gun above us,' someone whispered almost inaudibly.

A crunching noise came from the wall.

'Low-flying aircraft?'

Someone hissed: 'Stop talking'

Iron flaps in the wall sealed the air-slits in the concrete. One of them swung back with a crash. A hissing noise issued from the crack behind it. A woman gave a piercing scream. Everyone jumped from the benches. Three hundred people ducked. They wanted to get from the walls to the door. Benches toppled. People moved on the stairs.

'Silence!' bellowed the boy.

Silence fell. Three hundred people straightened their clothes. They stood the benches back up.

'Nothing happened,' said the boy. 'The air pressure opened a flap. That's all.' He shook his head. The fans hummed.

People looked at the floor in embarrassment. Everyone was silent, and then a man called out: 'It's all the fault of the damned Americans!'

A woman screeched: 'Absolutely right!'

'Lynch them,' a voice from a corner agreed. 'Any murdering pilot who gets shot down deserves to be lynched.'

The altar of the fatherland was made not of stone, but of rubble. On it the girl had lost her virginity and a litre of blood.

'Let's die together!' the man suggested

He turned around. His hands moved through the darkness. They stroked the girl's forehead and covered her eyes. As though caressing her they touched her throat.

'Please stop touching me,' pleaded the girl.

She thought: He wants to kill me, and the thought gave her the strength to speak. Exhaustion paralysed her limbs. Her muscles were weak. Her head drooped to one side. The man's hand fell on her shoulder. His voice said: 'If you want.' He was as apathetic as she was.

Something wet crept up from the floor through her clothes. She stretched out her arm, touched the earth, reached into a puddle. 'Water,' she whispered. 'Where's the water coming from?'

'I don't know.'

She asked: 'Are you asleep?'

'No,' replied the man. 'I'm just tired.'

'Please don't go to sleep.'

The man didn't reply. His breathing was shallow. When she reached for his face his mouth was open. Her fingers bumped against his teeth. She called feebly: 'Wake up!'

The man said nothing. His breathing had stopped. Like a clock that suddenly falls silent. His hand dropped from her shoulder.

'Wake up!' She imagined she was shouting, but it was only a whisper. Her voice faded away in the rubble.

Stones rattled through the darkness. With great difficulty she turned to one side. The ground was slippery. Earth got under her fingernails.

She repeated: 'Wake up.'

There was a groan. The man's body rolled into the gap between them. His arm pressed against her leg. When she pushed him away she touched his wrist. A slit ran from his thumb to his wrist. That was where the wetness was coming from.

XII

I, Anna Katharina Countess Baudin, born on 9 September 1900, had a son:

They were travelling through the Arctic Ocean. The squadron was running in line ahead. There was a submarine alarm, but the sea was calm. One ship after another, half a mile apart, cut through the water. Everyone was shivering, and it was as silent as a graveyard. Only at the stern was there the sound of waves. Spray glistened in the polar light. There was no one there to see how it happened. Only when he was swimming in the water – his life-jacket held him upright – did they notice.

A mate whistled.

It was those long notes that rang hollowly over the whole ship. The signal meant: man overboard.

They were the leading ship of the squadron, and he was already drifting far astern. They signalled with a flashlight. The next cruiser back replied. The signals ran along seven ships. Mute flashes of light over a cold sea. They decided his fate. Not a hand could stir for him. The admiral didn't want to take chances because of the submarines. They did one thing: those weird unfeeling whistles rang out. All hands to port! They lined up in parade formation. Each time a ship passed by they saluted him. Each time a row of a hundred men put their hands to their caps. That was how they paid him their last respects, and he was still alive. He dangled helplessly in the ice-cold water. He stared at those rigid floating fortresses. Six times hope drifted past him. He could make out the foam at the keel, and the way they were turning their heads towards him. Synchronised and obedient. But he was only a tiny point on a motionless surface, and he stayed behind until no one could see him any more.

That was my son.

'How do you know that?' asked the woman with the metal tooth.

'One of his comrades told me.' The nurse fell silent. The humming of the fans sounded as it always did. The boy leaned on the barrel, put his fingers to his teeth and looked into the corner. He listened. Dull thuds came from the door. Knocking.

'There's someone outside,' said the nurse.

'Do you think so?'

'Yes.'

The boy took his hand out of his mouth, and the woman walked to the door. She drew back the bolt. The hinges grated, smoke forced its way through the chink, and then in he came:

An animal walking upright. Glittering eyes under a layer of soot, naked from the waist down. He staggered in, saw the barrel and flung himself on it. His head disappeared into the water. The man gurgled.

The boy jumped aside with a shout. Fear gripped his throat like a hand. The figure over the barrel began to slurp.

'That,' the woman said, confused, 'is unhealthy.' But the man went on drinking. They stared at him. His bottom, his bare legs in his shoes, a belt around his naked hips. A woven leather strap from his holster beat against his thigh.

The boy whispered: 'An American.'

Steam rose up. In the dug-out the walls ran with water. Puddles formed on the floor. The wireless operator wiped his nose with his arm, smearing his sleeve. He rubbed the sleeve with the balls of his hands. Then the doorway darkened, and a woman walked in. Sweat was running down her face.

'Where's my boy?'

'What?'

The operator asked, startled: 'What boy?' Outside the salvoes were hurtling into the sky. He was almost screaming.

'Fischer!' The woman shouted: 'My name is Fischer!'

'Yes!'

'Where's my boy?'

The operator roared: 'Yes, Frau Fischer!' The blood rose to his head. He looked at the woman. The tatters of a coat hung from her body. She was wearing gloves. Her fingers poked through the fabric. The shoe was missing from her right foot. He had never seen this woman before.

'How on earth did you get here?' he blurted.

'On my bike.'

His mouth grew dry. 'Sit down.'

'Where,' wheezed the woman, 'where is my boy?'

'Gunner Fischer?'

The woman's face contorted. 'Did I speak to you on the phone?'

'No!'

'But it was your voice. He's wounded.'

The woman leaned against the wall. Arms dropped. She began to tremble with exhaustion. The foot in the shoe went over on its ankle. She fell to her knees. She immediately stood up again. She waved her hand feebly through the air. There were lines of dirt across from her forehead. 'Where is he, then?' she wailed. The guns in the emplacement fired. She looked towards the door with a hunted expression. 'Where is he?'

'I . . . We . . .' the operator stammered, 'Calm down, it's . . .'

'What?'

'Not as bad as you think.'

'Thank God.'

The woman began to sob. She put her face in her hands, smearing the dirt and tears over her cheeks. 'Can I see him? He's my only one!' She undid her headscarf with her hand, and used it to wipe away the sweat and tears. 'So how badly wounded is he?'

'Frau Fischer!' The operator looked at the floor. 'Your son is . . .'

'What?' the woman shouted.

'Isn't here any more!' The operator reached for a button on his shirt. He looked at his fingers. He had bitten off his nails. 'Isn't here any more.'

'Where is he?'

The operator raised his head. The woman looked at him, fear in her face. The skin was wrinkled around her neck. He whispered: 'He's . . .'

'Where?'

'Been moved!'

'Where to?'

'I can't . . .' The operator shook his head and turned away. 'I can't tell you..' His eye fell on the corner where the radios were. A bloody scrap of paper lay next to the receiver. He quickly walked over, stood by it and spread his arms out. It was as though he wanted to defend the paper.

'Where to?' The woman's eyes bulged.

'I don't know.'

'Phone them!'

'What?'

'Phone them!' The woman dashed towards him. The telephone was by his right arm. She grabbed the receiver. He banged his hand down on the cradle. Their hands touched. They stared at one another, then he breathed out and said: 'You can't do that.'

'Why not?'

'It's forbidden!'

His hand gripped the receiver.

'Then you call.' A breath of warm air struck his face. He saw little scratches on the woman's forehead. A small golden leaf hung from her ear. The stone had fallen from its setting. He asked: 'Me?'

'Yes!'

He pushed the woman's hand aside. 'Go to the door!'

'Why?' The woman was suspicious.

'It's secret!'

The woman sobbed. 'My son was only a gunner!' Her mouth stayed open. 'Is a gunner! Is! Is!' she stammered.

'Go to the door!'

'Soldier!'

'Excuse me,' the operator said, raising his arm. 'You'll get in my way if you stay here!' He shook his head vigorously. 'It's secret, very secret!'

The woman walked quickly to the door, and he slowly picked up the receiver. As he put it to his ear, she looked over, questioningly. Her face was half in shadow. He shouted into the mouthpiece: 'Switchboard?'

'Speaking,' a voice said quietly. He immediately pressed the receiver to his head. 'Where have the wounded been taken?' he asked loudly.

'What wounded?'

'Yes!' he shouted. 'Yes, quite right!'

'Wrong number!' There was a click.

'Yes sir!' He saw the woman's outline in the doorway. His hand was sticky. 'Two men!' he shouted. He shouted: 'From Saturn gun!'

'You fool,' a voice said. 'Have you lost your marbles?' He pulled up his tunic and held it over the receiver.

'Private Fischer!' the woman called to him. 'Gunner Fischer!'

He roared into the mouthpiece. 'Fischer is his name!'

'He has,' the woman cried, 'fair hair.'

The operator roared: 'Yes, thank you!' and quickly put the phone down. Sweat ran over his face. 'Auxiliary hospital on Bauderstrasse,' he said.

'Bauderstrasse!' The woman was about to turn around.

'Stop!'

She stood in the doorway and turned her head. A new salvo exploded outside. He shouted: 'Take this!' He pulled the iron cross from his trouser pocket and held it out to her. 'Your son was awarded this. First Class!' he said, with admiration in his voice, and pressed it into her hand. 'Give it to him.'

'Yes.'

The woman's lips moved. He thought he heard something but he didn't. They climbed the stairs. The coat flapped about her legs. Her stocking sagged on her shoeless foot. He wrung his hands. They were slippery.

He couldn't shake off the feeling of having plunged his hands into soft soap.

Herr Cheovski whispered: 'Dessy.'

The vault creaked. Rats flitted along the corridor. But there weren't any. It was only her ragged dress brushing on the floor. They both staggered.

'Dessy!'

A red light gleamed in the darkness. Relieved, he walked towards it and bumped into a bicycle. It fell over. The rear light broke from its fitting. It tumbled away over the stones.

'Dessy!' He ordered crossly: 'Answer me!'

'Where's the soldier?'

'Don't worry about the soldier. We've got to get out of here.' His hand touched her arm. A sickly scent flowed through the darkness. He could smell it quite distinctly. He felt his way towards the draught. He clutched her arm tightly. His other hand was stretched out in front of him.

'I don't think so.'

'What?'

'I don't think this is the way out.' Her voice sounded dull.

He answered loudly: 'But of course it is!'

He was startled at his tone. It was shrill. The floor hummed. With his next step his hand bumped against a wall. He whispered: 'We've taken a wrong turning.'

The stones were cold and slippery. But he was less disgusted than frightened.

'Along here.'

'No.'

Frau Cheovski said: 'Yes, you've got to follow me.'

He stepped on her dress. Fabric tore. She pulled him away.

'There!'

A draught blew into his face. Suddenly he bumped against wood. Now the cold was coming from the side. He groped his way across a wall. He asked: 'Can you find the way?'

'No, there's a wall here.'

'Back, then!'

Bombs swooshed above them. They whistled past. When they exploded not even the earth moved. Wheels ground in the distance.

'Come on!'

Hand in hand they walked towards where the draught was coming from. It grew louder. Hissed. They bumped into the wall together.

'Wrong!'

'But what's hissing?'

It was a pipe. When he reached for it he also found the opening. There was a gap somewhere. It was flowing from there.

'Gas?'

'No!'

'Yes it is, I can smell it!'

He turned around and pulled her with him. Their feet stepped over gravel. Stones buzzed like bees. His head crashed against wood. Rubble lay around and behind it. A cricket chirped somewhere on the ceiling.

He said: 'I'll guide you, just rely on me.'

'Yes.'

After precisely six paces he tripped over the bicycle and dragged her down with him.

'This proves . . .' The doctor gave a ringing laugh, 'that it isn't just bombs that rain from the sky, ghosts do, too!' He grabbed the figure by the hand and pushed it away from him. It fell on its back. Strenehen fell on to the stretcher. He thought: I've found my father. At last.

His features changed to a smile. He forgot fire and smoke. He was at home here.

'*Hello there!*'

The doctor kicked over the stretcher. Strenehen rolled across the floor. Happiness filled him like a dream. His mother was standing by the wall. He thought: She won't abandon me.

'My good man!' called the doctor. 'No sleeping here, arise, shake off the dream of night! Shakespeare, more or less!'

He pushed his foot against a chair. The chair toppled into Strenehen's face. Stars flickered before his eyes. He got to his feet. Ponderous as a bear.

'What I need now,' whispered the doctor, 'is a whip.'

A voice shouted: 'No!'

It was the nurse. She was standing by the door. Walls spun around her. The boy peeped out behind her, eyes like head-lights. He whispered: 'Kill him.'

The nurse opened her coat and took it off. She walked over to Strenehen and wrapped him up. He thought: Thank you, mother. He gave her a friendly smile. A grimace under a layer of soot. The nurse gave a start.

'A whip,' said the doctor. 'Bring me one.'

'Doctor!' The boy came from the door. In his hands he carried a poker. He tripped over his feet, straightened up again and handed it to the doctor.

'Terrific!'

The doctor struck at Strenehen's shoulder with the poker. A bone cracked. The boy thought: So that's how you do it.

'Down with innocence!'

The iron got caught in the coat. He pulled it off Strenehen's body. Material sank to the floor like a carapace. Father, thought Strenehen, as long as I'm with you!

'Gangster!'

The poker touched Strenehen's genitals.

'What noble prey have you felled with that?'

The iron was cold. Strenehen giggled. Metallic sounds.

'Stop it!'

'No!' There was foam on the doctor's lips. 'Has no one here got a bib? Let the monkey do some work!'

'Yes sir!' Light fell on the boy's red hair. His head disappeared behind the door.

The nurse's voice said: 'I'm going to report everything I've seen here.'

'To whom?'

Laughter rang up to the ceiling. The doctor and Strenehen laughed together. The skin tightened over Strenehen's belly. This is my home, he thought. I am happy.

The doctor stopped. 'Yankee pig!'

'Stop it!'

The poker flew at Strenehen's legs. It made a clinking noise.

'Here's an apron!' The boy stood in the doorway. He held a white cloth in his hands.

'Tie it around him!'

The boy stepped forward. He stood behind Strenehen and put the apron over his belly.

'Higher!' ordered the doctor. 'Let everyone see his prick.'

'Stop it!'

'No!'

The boy obeyed.

'Give me the holster. I want the memory of this encounter to be a precious one.'

'Yes, sir!' The boy took the belt off Strenehen and handed it over.

'Nicely done. Now turn him around.'

The boy pulled Strenehen by the arm until he was facing the door. 'Careful!' The doctor became aroused. He raised his foot. The nurse covered her eyes with her hands.

'A free citizen of the United States,' said the doctor, 'greets you!' With these words he kicked Strenehen in the buttocks. The figure went flying to the door and staggered out.

'Into the day-rooms with him!'

The boy roared: 'Look out, here comes a Yankee pig!'

Father, thought Strenehen, what are you doing to me?

XIII

I, Egon Michael, M.D., born on 30 January 1901, studied in Tübingen.

Our father, a consul in Hamburg, saw to it that we had a good education. Thus, for example, I remember that he would talk to us for a while each day after dinner. He always treated me, in particular, as an adult. We were utterly unfamiliar with discipline in the sense of punishment. It was in keeping with our social position that we were made to learn several languages, play the piano and mind our manners. At the time, the friends who came to our house included not only influential public figures, but also famous scientists and artists. My father was without prejudices of any kind. While my brothers and sisters devoted themselves to simpler pleasures, even at the age of fifteen I was reading medical texts. Today I am convinced that even at that early age I was expressing the desire to achieve something in this field. Only my mother always observed my inclinations with some suspicion. I might mention that she was a simple, quiet woman, who did not, perhaps, fit into the milieu in which our family moved. She died young, something that I of course very much regretted.

'Now,' the lance corporal explained, 'I'm going to rest my tired arse against the wall for a bit.' He closed the door behind him. The soldiers were standing in the air-lock. One of them spat. The mucus fell right in the middle of the barrel. Before it vanished in the water it spun in a circle.

'God you're a pig.'

The soldier who had spat gave an embarrassed laugh. Steel helmets rolled across the floor. The men's weapons clanked. One by one they squatted down.

'They could tie a naked woman to my belly right now,' said the adolescent-sounding voice, 'and I wouldn't be interested. I'm too tired.'

The fans hummed. Matches were lit. The plaster gleamed on the walls. A cigarette was passed around.

'Mum, is there a toilet somewhere?' called the soldier with the freckles. He stood up again. 'I'm bursting!'

'Aha!' answered someone triumphantly. 'Now I know why it stinks in here!'

'Shut up!'

The voice came from the corner. A woman stepped forward. She opened her mouth. The soldiers' heads turned towards her. They studied her metal tooth with great interest. The woman asked: 'Where's your officer?'

'Lutz!' The childish face twisted into a smile. 'You're wanted on the phone!' Giggles suddenly rose up and faded away again. One of the men burped. The ensign turned his head: 'What do you want from me?'

'You're no officer,' the woman answered. 'You're drunk.'

'Hello!'

Rifle-butts struck the concrete. Someone banged his steel helmet against the wall. A voice grunted: 'Officer or not. A word from him. We're organising a slaughter-party.'

The woman blinked. 'Are you in charge of this mob?'

'Yes,' said the ensign, 'if you don't mind.'

'Then stand up. I've got to talk to you.'

'Did you hear that?' asked the lance corporal. 'She called us a mob.'

The ensign put his gun on the concrete and got to his feet. He walked through the seated men to the woman. His hair stuck to his head. His helmet still lay on the floor. When he was standing in front of her the woman started whispering.

There was giggling. One of the soldiers called quietly: 'Fancy a bit?' Someone stuck his legs awkwardly into the room.

The woman went on whispering. As she spoke, the ensign turned around with a jerk and looked at the door that led to the bunker.

'Louder!' demanded the lance corporal.

Cigarette smoke drifted towards the doorway. Behind the barrel someone started snoring.

'Damn!' cried the soldier with the freckles. 'Could somebody please tell me where the toilet is here?'

He held his hands in front of his belly and looked at the ceiling.

The ensign suddenly asked loudly: 'Is what you're telling me true?'

The woman answered just as loudly: 'May God be my judge!'

'A gun!'

The lance corporal asked: 'What did you say?'

'Give me your gun!'

The lance corporal reached to his hip, pulled out his weapon and held it in the air. The ensign came up to him through the others. He took it out of his hand.

'Careful!' the lance corporal warned. 'The thing's loaded.'

'You wait here till I get back.' The safety catch clicked on the gun. The ensign climbed between two pairs of legs, tripped over a rifle and finally reached the door.

The girl fell asleep. The tension ebbed from her face, and it began to resemble the photograph that a certain soldier had received from her. Perhaps, surrounded by rubble, and beneath the dull whirling impacts of the bombs, she was recalling something stronger than terror. The three timid words at the end of the last letter that she had written and the one she had received.

Sand trickled on to her abdomen and tried to cover up what had happened to her. With her final movement she folded her hands. Weariness swept through her body. She went to sleep like that. The earth trembled beneath her. Rubble shifted. She was no longer touching anything.

*

Strenehen swayed into the room, spun around and stopped. Pebbles scattered beneath his feet. The apron hung open over his chest. It hung like a bib from throat to hip.

A child's voice demanded: 'Kill him!'

People raised their heads. Eyes stared at him. A corridor opened up before him. Movement ran through the ranks. A man stood up and called out: 'Who's that?'

'An American!'

Silence descended. Wood creaked. A coin fell to the floor in a corner. It rolled over the concrete.

'Kill him!'

The fans hissed. Strenehen took a step forward. A woman started back. She stretched her hands out defensively. Her mouth contorted. But she said nothing. Strenehen saw two hands.

'Kill him!'

The boy was standing at the door. His pimpled chin gleamed. A beam of light fell into his eyes. It was the indifferent face of a child torturing an animal. He braced his arms against his hips and said: 'If you're afraid of him, I'll have to do it myself.'

There was more movement on the stairs. Men pushed their way in. Strenehen fell on his knees and got to his feet again. He turned around and stood with his face to the door. No one moved.

'Kill the gangster!'

Someone put a suitcase on the floor. An adolescent voice bellowed: 'Shut that boy up!'

Strenehen stepped backwards. The cry faded away behind him. He suddenly covered his genitals with both hands. The boy at the door clenched his fist and lifted his arm.

'Kill the . . .'

An arm was laid around the boy's throat. A hand blocked his mouth. He was pushed back. He disappeared behind the figure of a woman.

A voice called: 'Take his apron off!'

'Put a blanket around him,' said another voice. Someone stepped forward. A woman. She walked over to Strenehen and unbuttoned his apron. Her hands were trembling. The white apron sank to the floor. Feet pushed it aside. Strenehen raised his face to the lamp that hung over him. He stood in a circle of beams.

'Here!'

Something grey flew through the air. A blanket. Arms caught it. Strenehen swayed. A man came over with the blanket and wrapped him up. He sank to the floor. Strenehen's right hand slapped on the concrete.

'I'm ashamed,' said a voice from the wall, 'of whoever it was who did that.'

Strenehen rolled on to his side in the blanket. His eyes closed. Startled, the man put his hand to his forehead.

'Water!' came the cry from the stairs.

The man straightened and looked at the door. Into a motionless silence, his voice said: 'He's died.'

'Murder!'

A sob came from the crowd.

The woman who had unbuttoned Strenehen's apron looked around and folded her hands. She began quietly: 'Our father, which art in Heaven . . .'

They rose from their benches. Men took off their hats. The light was reflected in someone's bald patch.

★

The ensign quietly pushed open the door to the dressing station with the barrel of his gun. He saw a man's back. His face was turned to the wall. A white coat hung over his shoulder. The beam of light fell on his boots. They gleamed.

'Turn round,' said the ensign.

Startled, the man turned his head. He was about to shout something, but his mouth stayed shut.

'Michael,' blurted the ensign. 'Is it you or isn't it?'

'It's me!'

'Now,' answered the ensign, 'I nearly . . .' He stopped, put the safety catch on the gun and put it in his pocket.

'Lutz, man, let's have a look at you!' The doctor stepped forward and gripped the ensign by the hands. 'This calls for a drink!'

'My opinion entirely.'

'Wait!'

The doctor went to the wall, opened a little cupboard and took out a bottle and two glasses. He handed one to the ensign.

'Moselle?'

The doctor laughed. 'My favourite tipple!'

He filled the glass. There was a duelling scar on his cheek.

'If you knew,' said the ensign.

'What?'

'How much I've drunk already today.'

The doctor cried cheerfully: 'One good piss-up deserves another. What shall we drink to?'

'To old comrades!'

The doctor put his glass to his lips and knocked it back. 'Cheers!' He drank the wine as though it was water.

'Cheers!' The ensign swallowed, wiped his mouth and laughed. He said: 'You haven't changed.'

'Me!' The doctor filled the glass again. 'I'll never change.' Some wine splashed on the floor.

'What shall we drink to now?' asked the ensign.

'To the sight of a battlefield at dawn'

The ensign swayed slightly. He rolled his eyes. His face reddened. 'That's shit.'

'No, it isn't!' The doctor drained his glass and grew cheerful. 'Have you never seen such a thing?'

'Yes, I have,' answered the ensign. 'But all I could ever see was the battlefield.' He sipped from his glass and started shaking.

'Drink up.'

'Cheers!' As he was too exhausted to clink glasses with the doctor, he tapped on his glass with his finger.

'As far as I'm concerned,' cried the doctor, and raised the bottle against the light, 'war is the father of all things!'

He filled the glasses again.

'It crystallises my values. As far as I'm concerned it's salvation and experience, a means to a political end or something the situation calls for. Courage overcomes my fear. I find the sight of a battlefield at dawn uplifting.'

'Be quiet!' The ensign turned around. He stammered: 'What's that?' He stood on the concrete. Murmurs came from behind the door.

'We'll soon find out.' The doctor stepped forward and pulled the door open. Their arms touched. They held the full wineglasses in their hands and listened.

'. . . and forgive us our trespasses,' people somewhere were saying in chorus, 'as we forgive those who trespass against us.'

The chorus paused, and one clear voice continued: 'For they know not what they do.'

And suddenly the chorus continued as well: 'For they know not what they do. Amen.'

Central European time: 14:10

God on our side.

But he was on the others' side as well. In the seventieth minute of the raid the bomb-sights of the third wave of bombers unleashed forty air-mines.

Stones shot into the sky like rockets. The wooden crosses in the graveyard had already burned to ashes. In the wrecked station waiting-room bleeding children crept over stone steps. In a church bombs pulled Christ from the cross, in the cellar of the maternity home they tore the soft skin from the heads of the babies, somewhere a woman's folded hands were torn apart, and in the zoo's outdoor enclosure monkeys were ripped from the trees where they had sought refuge.

The painting of a Madonna was pulled from its frame, the manuscript of a saint was blown away and a living man's leg was scorched.

Progress destroyed both past and future. Within an hour children lost their mother and Maria Erika Weinert her life.

She didn't get a medal for it. Someone found that unjust.

During that hour, on the other hand a mother looking for her son, who had vanished for ever, got her cross.

She spent ten years looking for her son, and then she died.

A week later a minister visited the Strenehen family at their gas station between Dallas and Forth Worth. The man claimed: 'The Lord gives and the Lord takes away, just as he pleases.' And everything would be for the best. If someone is missing, it means they haven't been killed yet.

At the end of that hour about three hundred people were missing. Twelve were found.

They found Sam Ohm in the afternoon. They claimed his skin was charred. Someone saw the pink patches on the insides of his hands and called him a nigger. A boy with pimples on his chin immediately stamped on his head.

An officer told a woman: your son died fulfilling his duty as a hero.

Three days later the dead man wrote: No, we are not in the city, Mother. Do I have to keep repeating that?

An hour was all it took for terror to triumph. Afterwards some people wanted to forget that fact. Others claimed not to have known it. It seems they hadn't been able to do anything about it.

After the seventieth minute the bombing resumed. Payback was doing its work.

It was unstoppable.

It just wasn't the Day of Judgment.

THE HOTHOUSE
A Novel

Wolfgang Koeppen
Translated and introduced by Michael Hofmann

The Hothouse refers to the city of Bonn, with its warm damp climate, but it also refers to the political environment of the capital of divided Germany, where politics in the 1950s was about compromises, half measures and convenient forgetfulness. The central character, Keetenheuve, is an idealistic politician-intellectual who has returned from voluntary exile during the Nazi period. Now his idealism becomes a trap for him, as he attempts to break with the past and persuade his colleagues to embrace a radical rejection of militarism. The novel traces the final two days in the life of this depressed, isolated man.

'A mid-20th century masterpiece . . . a nihilist, mock-Wagnerian reflection on the unacknowledged corruption of post-war Germany' Stevie Davies, *Independent on Sunday Books of the Year*

'A marvellous discovery of a writer I had never heard of' Nadine Gordimer, *Times Literary Supplement*

'Muscular, elegant prose . . . Koeppen's writing is a revelation, dense with controlled, scathing anger and bitter insights'
The Times

TEETH AND SPIES

Giorgio Pressburger

Translated by Shaun Whiteside

This is the tragi-comic account of one man's life through the fate of his teeth; from the loss of his first milk tooth swallowed by his father in a prison camp, to the eventual fixture of a set of dentures. Devoting each chapter to a particular tooth, the unnamed narrator charts fifty years of East European history.

'Beautifully written, often moving and disturbing' *Observer*

'An intriguing and highly original account of some of the most perplexing issues of our time' *Times Literary Supplement*

'Who would have dreamt that there would be such poetry in teeth, such scope for meditation on the profoundest moments of a life? Woven into his story are major events of recent European history and philosophical reflections' *The Age*

COLLECTED SHORTER FICTION OF JOSEPH ROTH

Translated by Michael Hofmann

'Joseph Roth's literary reputation is undergoing a welcome revival in this country. This is largely thanks to his English translator Michael Hofmann. The seventeen stories testify to Roth's remarkable talent. It is hard to define the strange quality of Roth's genius . . . ordinary words are what his fiction is about – his stories are elegant, realist fables written in laconic prose. Every line is concretely realised and Roth is a mesmerising writer . . . this is fiction at its best – so real, it is magical. These stories are not overtly political. But they illustrate how in life the individual is invariably defeated: by the state, by fate, by a lover. The collection demonstrates Roth's versatility and his genius' *Literary Review*

'In German-speaking countries, Joseph Roth is counted among the great novelists of the twentieth century'
Times Literary Supplement

'The poet Michael Hofmann has performed such an invaluable service that it's a shame that the minting of medals has gone out of fashion. He has rescued from oblivion the works of one of the greatest European writers of the twentieth century, Joseph Roth, who is finally beginning to gain the serious attention he deserves'
Evening Standard

THE WANDERING JEWS

Joseph Roth

Translated by Michael Hofmann

The great novelist Joseph Roth, in the last years of Weimar Germany, set out to explore the Jewish communities scattered across Europe and America. He brought back reports of hope, poverty, fear and persecution. He witnessed the twilight years of the *shtetls* and schools of Eastern Europe, and foresaw the dangers posed by extreme German nationalism.

This is the first translation of Roth's non-fiction to appear in English.

'*The Wandering Jews* reconnects with the rich complexities of European Jewish culture before it was swallowed up by the Holocaust. Roth's brilliant and penetrating analysis proved tragically prophetic. At this distance, it gives a timeless perspective on the vulnerability of dispossessed people everywhere' *The Times*

'His journalism is impressionistic, poetic, beautifully phrased. The world he describes is a reality observed with the eye and heart of a novelist' *Independent*

'One of the literary masters of the 20th century' *Sunday Times*

'Read everything he has written – and wonder at one of literature's most enduring, beguiling and deserving voices' Eileen Battersby, *Irish Times*